FRED

Buffalo Building of Dreams

A Novel

by Frances R. Schmidt

"I've witnessed the tragedies, joys, hopes, and dreams of my treasured tenants and their families. They've shown what it takes to thrive and survive in America."

~ FRED

Praise for Fred's Author
Frances R. Schmidt

Through the eyes and ears of "Fred," we see the hopes and struggles endured by those who came searching for a better life. The novel, beautifully created, by author Frances Schmidt, paints a picture that encompasses multiethnic groups and those of color alike. It's a reminder to us, their descendants, to reflect on their toils and not cast aside those who come today searching for the same dream.

Joseph Di Leo, Publisher
Per Niente Magazine

FRED: Buffalo Building of Dreams *gives new meaning to the expression "if walls could talk." In Schmidt's novel, they actually do, telling the story of Buffalo through the eyes of a 120-year-old building. Along the way, we learn about the lives of a bevy of characters of all races and creeds, teaching us not only about life on one city block but of human civilization in a century of immense change and loss. Bravo to Schmidt for reminding us just how rich in history Buffalo truly is.*

Rabbi Alexander Lazarus-Klein
Congregation Shir Shalom

This is a fascinating walk down Buffalo's past. The characters are interesting, colorful, and historic. The author has taken memorable moments that highlight the Queen City as seen through the eyes of an aging apartment building. It is an emotional read as you follow the lives of its tenants. Full of romance, intrigue, and heartfelt stories. As you read, you become familiar and attached to the residents. Telling the stories through the eyes of the building's life is creative and imaginative. The building actually takes on a life of its own. If you've never been to Buffalo, you'll feel as if you've lived here your whole life. It truly depicts the spirit of the "City of Good Neighbors."

Michaelene Karpinski
Administrative Assistant to the President of Villa Maria College

It's fascinating. I was captivated from the beginning. The story of Fred is difficult to stop reading. There is so much history in the life of one building. It really makes you think about so many things. I recommend this as a wonderful read that will broaden your viewpoint on history and especially the many lives that come into our neighborhoods.

John Brands, Jr.
Operations Manager, Santasiero's Restaurant

It's not often a building tells a story, and rarer still when that story both spans a city's history and is told by the building itself. With a unique voice and perspective, Fred provides a romp through Buffalo's history through the experiences and stories of the many tenants that have occupied his walls over the years. As the times change, so too do the tenants and residents, and we follow along with births, deaths, marriages, meetings of suffragettes and professors, all the way to the modern rebirth of Niagara Street and Buffalo's West Side.

Anyone who has spent a decent amount of time on the West Side is most likely familiar with the building and its many guises throughout the years, and through a detailed and well-researched history of its tenants, the author brings the past to life in a most novel method, centering around a structure of many lives perched on the edge of the Niagara.

Fans of American history, architecture, and Buffalo alike will find joy in sharing the life of a building that has stood through ups and downs and housed dozens of Buffalonians past.

Jason Barone
Manager of Isais Gonzalez-Soto Branch Library

The building of a community emerges with the construction of Fred, a commercial building and our storyteller who shares the lives of his tenants with us. We learn of the love entanglements of Fred's builder, Leon, and the societal judgments of out of wedlock children. Struggles to find employment and jobs that paid a decent rate were shared whether the family name was Murphy, Torres, or Henson. The reader can feel the joy of the Jablonski family as they move from an apartment and purchase their own home. Sunday dinners, a handwritten diary, protests, wars, religious diversity, sponsoring relatives, and sending money back home all bring back memories of my growing up in South Buffalo. I could smell the aroma of our own family dinners as Fred tells us about the Schiavone's preparations for their "extra special" Sunday dinner. Memories of the New York Central Terminal brought back visions of welcoming relatives who had been sponsored and then became part of our immediate family. There always seemed to be room for one more.

As the building evolves and community changes, we see many recurring themes. Is this 2021 or 1940? Has society changed much or are we still dealing with the lack of equality, fairness, respect, and opportunity just as Fred witnessed through his tenants? The cohesive families of Fred's early years and their network of support seems to be lost in our time. The stale Irish stereotype of drinking was a disappointment, but the flavor and ethnic diversity Fred enjoyed brought back memories of a time when we knew that we were all part of the tapestry that created our community.

FRED: Buffalo Building of Dreams will be enjoyed by all who want to get a better understanding of the immigrant experience or just want to reminisce about growing up in Buffalo.

Mary C. Heneghan
Chairman, Buffalo Irish Center

With each chapter, I found myself anxiously wondering who was moving in next and what their story was. If every building in Buffalo had a biography such as this, I wonder if we would be so quick to tear so much of our history down, if we may appreciate the lesson each story and each tenant could bring us. I am quickly reminded that we are stewards of our built environment; we should conserve their embodied energy and nurture their stories, saved for generations after we're gone. I wish Fred another 100 years demolition-free and I'm sad I won't be around to read about his next century of tenants, their struggles, hardships, and triumphs.

> *Christina Lincoln*
> *Housing Rehab Programs Manager for the Matt Urban Center/*
> *Co-chair of the Fillmore*
> *Forward Design Committee*

I most appreciated Chapters 20, 21, and 22 with arguably one of the most divided presidential elections. I found comfort in your allyship. When someone can understand the root of a social group's pain, that is when true allyship and compassion manifest. You have made it clear your interests and belief in sharing the story of many people and for this, I am grateful. I am confident other readers will feel the same.

> *Joshua Charles*
> *Cornell University|College of Agriculture and Life Sciences '20*
> *Interdisciplinary Studies in Economic Development*

ISBN (Print): 978-1-09835-494-7
ISBN (eBook): 978-1-09835-495-4

DEDICATION

· · · · · · · · · · · ·

This historical fiction novel is dedicated to Lillie Rosanna Sharon, my mother and best friend, and Frank Santora for their wisdom, encouragement, and contribution to this project, including Brother Jim Sarach, a living legacy, and in the memory of Margaret Clark and Ted Van Duesen, Back on Track Volunteers unsung heroes, including Patricia Yeager Fred's friend.

CONTENTS

· · · · · · · · · ·

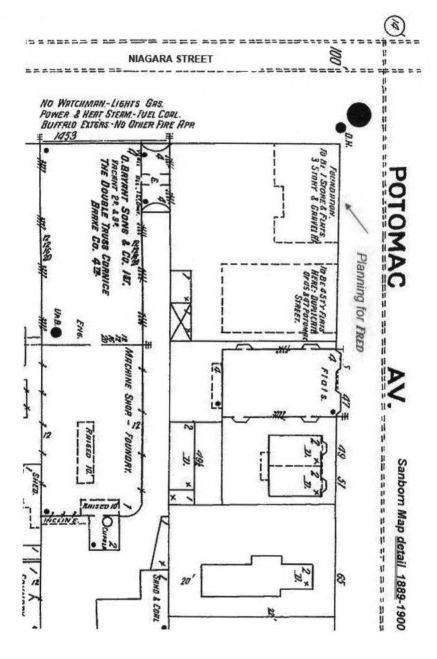

Sanborn Map Buffalo 1889–1900, Vol. 4 Sheet 327, detail.
Buffalo Public Library, Research Databases, Sanborn Maps.

CHAPTER ONE

· · · · · · · · · · · · ·

Fred

I don't remember the exact day, but I do know it was in the spring of 2006 when she first drove by the corner of my busy street. "Please tell my story," I pleaded, "before it's too late." For the first time, I thought maybe someone heard me because her black Toyota slowed down and she turned her head, briefly staring at me.

Year after year, I waited for her to come back. Then in 2012, she returned and parked in front of me.

In the beginning, I was called Building 1469 and my author called me an orphan because I was in terrible condition. Early on, my name was given to me by her childhood friend who has been able to connect with the past. Having a name and being valued by a stranger is powerful. But what I've learned over the past hundred and twenty-one years is that you can never underestimate anyone's history, including mine.

We all have stories to tell, and I am lucky to be alive to share mine. I am one out of thousands of apartment buildings throughout America with untold stories. Many of my wealthy counterparts are lucky because their histories are already valued. My stories have been lost in the shuffle of time. I often ask myself why are they important?

Maybe it's because I'm among the oldest apartment buildings still standing on the West Side of Buffalo, New York.

Recently, many of "Fred's Friends" have emerged to tell stories of their experiences in my building and neighborhood. These friends are a core group of people who believe it is my mission to share my tales. They also include former neighbors who lived across or down the street from me decades ago and were all interviewed by Fran, my author, and her researchers. Each person they talked to had agreed to become one of "Fred's Friends."

I'd describe myself as a modest four-story apartment building licensed to have a business on the first floor, along with a separate apartment. There are two apartments on each of my top three floors. My architecture is early Twentieth Century Commercial style. I am plain, with a flat appearance and panels of light-colored brick laid in patterns. I've been able to provide my tenants shelter, a little space, and some comfort. There have been love affairs, reunions, and heroism within my walls. I've witnessed the tragedies, joys, hopes, and dreams of my tenants and their families. I learned that it doesn't matter who we are or where we come from, we all have experiences to share.

As I grew older, I felt compelled to tell my story. Sometimes it was sad to see what became of me in my later years. In recent decades, I've been vulnerable to the weather and been a victim of many thefts to my structural integrity. My copper pipes have been ripped out, and the hole in my roof has damaged my interior. The traffic on Niagara Street comes and goes, mostly in a hurry, and now two new billboards clinging to the right-hand side of me generate income for my latest owner. At one point, vandals spray-painted my front bay windows in the middle of the night, but I'm still lucky because my legacy continues struggling to survive.

Young preservationists *heart-bombed* me on Valentine's Day 2013 with paper hearts because I was a member of the city's most endangered buildings in desperate need of tender, loving care. This young group of advocates are heroes because they continue to educate the public on why many of our buildings and neighborhoods need to be saved. I'm lucky I made it on their list and was considered valuable and worth protecting for future generations. They have no idea how much I appreciate their efforts or maybe they will when they read this novel. My bay windows still have their flush lintels and protruding sills, and I am still strong with my three-foot-thick concrete basement walls and mostly solid original roof. Being heart-bombed made me feel important and brought back memories of someone special.

While I was being built, a young woman with a little boy cradled in her arms often stood in front of me, silently watching. Sometimes she talked briefly with the laborers and the builder, and I don't know how it happened, but I felt her affection toward me.

Whenever it rained or snowed, or if we had high winds, I'd see her sitting and looking out the window of the home nearest to my vacant side lot. I saw her smile and talk to her small child while pointing in my direction. Little did I know she would become my first owner—her name was Abigail.

It wasn't long before I referred to her as My Dear Abigail. Little did she know that when she was standing in front of me being built, I heard what she said out loud to her child. It was the beginning of my ability to listen and observe many of my tenants' lives without their knowledge. When Abigail looked up at me, she said, "You're my independence, hope, and financial security." I was shocked and desperately wanted to answer her, but it was impossible.

Later, I discovered she had me built on a wing and a prayer, and without her, maybe I wouldn't still exist.

I'll never forget the day I was completed. It was later in the morning when I saw Abigail in her open window, crying and hugging her child. It was a great day when she moved into one of my third-floor apartments. Later, I learned that she'd paid $1,200 for the parcel of land and $6,000 for my apartment building. She was twenty-nine years old when my life began.

It's strange and exciting to be able to relate to my author. I wasn't only a singular apartment building. Through research and personal interviews by her and her researchers, they learned of my identical, narrow twin buildings that were constructed right next to me the year after I was built. I didn't really become an orphan until the 1950s when one of my twin buildings was set on fire and burned to the ground. A few years later, my surviving twin building was demolished. I'll never forget how we originally all stood out proudly in our residential neighborhood.

My apartment building faces Niagara Street on the corner of Potomac Avenue, and in the 1900s, Buffalo was booming and rapidly growing, including my neighborhood on the West Side. Luckily, I'm built next to the sidewalk's edge. It's the best of both worlds—living in a residential and industrial neighborhood.

I learned that what I do is called telepathy. It allows me to be able to communicate back and forth with Fran and her childhood friend, Mary, with the exception of one other person. My "Orphan Building" research team assists and does all the leg work along with my author and gathers feedback from the growing list of "Fred's Friends." We spent significant hours at the Buffalo Public Library researching who my original architect, builder, and owners were.

Their excitement and enthusiasm are contagious, and I can't wait for you to learn about my tenants.

Before we continue, I have to tell you about Edward F. Pickett, my architect, who was forty-two years old when he was hired to build me. He was a confident, spunky short first-generation Irish American. Edward's parents immigrated to New York City from Limerick, Ireland, in 1858. Edward's father worked as a laborer and his mother as a seamstress before they moved to Buffalo when he was two years old.

Jobs were plentiful in Buffalo, and the Pickett family wanted to save enough money to buy a house of their own. Edward's father, Patrick, easily found work with the Buffalo Street Railway Company. It wasn't long before his strong work ethic and willingness to work long hours enabled him to save enough money to purchase a two-family home on West Avenue.

Little Edward grew up to be just like his father and always challenged himself. He was a go-getter, and by 1895, he was employed by Bull and Brown, a local bicycle manufacturer located on Main and Chippewa Streets in the city of Buffalo. There, he became a department manager, a skilled bicycle machinist, and an inventor with many bicycle-related patents to his name. By 1896, he was vice president and secretary of the Non-Punctural Tire Company. Within a year, he was a draftsman for the Great Northern Elevator Company, a grain storage facility.

How Edward became Abigail's architect is an interesting tale. In the spring of 1898, Edward traveled by ferry to Fort Erie, Canada, for a large family reunion with all his Canadian relatives. By chance, he met Leon Edward O'Shannon, an Irish builder and friend of a distant cousin. They liked each other instantly because of their mutual love of bicycle touring. Before the reunion was over, both men agreed to meet in Buffalo and planned on touring together on their identical Columbia bicycles.

On their first tour together, they traveled the road to Alden, mainly because it was straight and one of the best roads leading out of Buffalo. They continued to Warsaw and then took the road west of the Erie Railroad, which was always hard, smooth, and flat.

Little did they know that on their first tour together they would meet Louise Blanchard Bethune, the first woman architect in America. It was a beautiful day, and Edward, Leon, and Louise ended up sharing lunch together. They found out that Louise had bought the first woman's bicycle to go on sale in Buffalo and that she was an active member of the Woman's Wheel and Athletic Club. They had so much fun together that the three of them made sure to schedule more tours together.

In 1876, Louise took a job working as a draftsman in the local office of Richard A. Waite and F. W. Caulky, along with her husband Robert Bethune, before becoming an official architect herself five years later. Edward had a lot in common with Louise, mainly because they both learned the art of architecture while working inside a firm instead of inside a classroom.

Meeting Louise was a great diversion for both men, and they enjoyed seeing their new friend occasionally on the same bicycle tour. Actually, it's how they all became good friends. It also enabled Leon to discuss Abigail Goodwin's dilemma. He confided in Edward and asked him if he could please consider helping his best friend's sister. Leon explained that Abigail's husband, John, had returned to his family's farm on the Isle of Wight in England to care for his elderly parents, and his wife, Abigail, refused to go. He'd arrived in England right before she found out she was pregnant with his child. John sent her money monthly for a while but suddenly stopped. It was when Abigail decided to buy an apartment building in Buffalo, New York, right over the border from Canada. She planned to rent an apartment in Buffalo until she could buy a building for herself.

Leon then told Edward that Abigail had been happy in Canada and never wanted to return to England with her husband and that he never wanted to return to America. John never forgave her for not returning to England with him and asked her for a divorce. When Abigail's Aunt Lillie died suddenly, she left her a considerable amount of money, saving her from poverty. It was then that she begged Leon to help her start a new life of independence in Buffalo, New York.

. . . .

CHAPTER TWO

Meet the Trailblazers

Abigail's family immigrated to Quebec, Canada, from Liverpool, England in 1871 when she was a baby. Her Papa, Edmond Goodwin, got a job working in Leno's Butcher Shop because he didn't have enough money saved to buy his own shop. The butcher was a good man and let Abigail's father take extra scraps and cuts of older meats home. Her father would sometimes pay Mr. Leno eight cents for mutton for a special dinner. But Abigail's father was dead-tired and angry all the time. He resented the fact that he had no sons who would be able to help him support the family and help him run a shop of his own.

Abigail's mother, Stephanie, was quiet and soft-spoken. She was a good woman who never stopped grieving Abigail's stillborn baby sister, Betty Anne. She left home every day before dawn to clean the house of a wealthy family friend of Mr. Leno. After supper, she continued working at home, helping a seamstress by mending clothes three evenings a week. She also taught Abigail to help her mend socks and clothing.

There was little conversation in her childhood home. Her mother did the best she could but never had time for herself or Abigail.

As a child, Abigail loved going to school and learning how to read and write. She constantly raised her hand and asked questions in class, but she knew better than to ask questions at home.

She left school at fourteen to work in a shirt factory, working long hours with little time for herself. When Abigail did have free time at home, she'd go to her bedroom, lie on her bed, and read all the fliers she had collected regarding the suffrage movement and their support of a woman's right to vote. Suffragettes gave her something important to think about. Hearing this made me wonder who the suffragettes were, and I couldn't wait to find out. Abigail imagined being saved from a wretched life under the control of others. In her mind, she was going to be a high school graduate and own an income property. She longed for freedom and independence.

When she was home, there was never time for family or friends, only working, sleeping, cleaning, and church on Sundays. They were a family in name only. Abigail felt lonely. There was no hugging, smiling, or friendly conversations, with only one exception: when she cleaned up the kitchen after their Sunday dinner, she was allowed to go to the park near her home for a couple of hours. There she'd take a walk, read a book, and watch people. I tried to imagine what it must have been like growing up with few, if any, choices. Actually, I'm describing myself because I can't make choices about my future.

During her weekly quiet time in the park, she'd often see a man sitting alone on a bench directly across from hers. He'd read the newspaper and sometimes smile at her. He was a trim, attractive older man with a full head of grayish hair. He looked like a kind man, not like her father. One day, he introduced himself to her. "Hello, miss," he said. "May I come sit and talk to you?" With a nod, Abigail agreed. Then, little by little, they became friends and made it a point to meet in the park every week. His name was Leon Edward O'Shannon.

Immediately, she felt a connection to him. He was the first and only man who ever interested her, even though he was forty-one, which was much older than Abigail's age. After many weeks of talking, Leon confided in her. "Abigail, I have to tell you something, but please hear me out without running away. Please promise me."

"I'll try."

"I'm in love with you with all my heart. I know I'm older, but I promise you my love will last a lifetime." He paused. "But . . . I'm married." Abigail's eyes opened wide and tears welled up in her eyes. "Please, please let me explain. I want to tell you everything about why I'm married."

Leon told her about the first time he met Anna, his wife, and her children. It happened when he was hired as the builder of her new home. She told him that her husband was out of the country on business. She was the one who worked closely with him during the entire building process. What I'm telling you, sweetheart, may sound unbelievable, but it's true" Leon said.

Later, Anna told Leon she had been married for five years and was ten years older than her husband. She was at the building site with her three small children almost every day.

When her house was almost finished, she stopped by alone without her children and was nervous and fidgety. She said, "Leon, I don't know what to do. I found out something terrible about my husband. I trust you, and we have become good friends. You've been a gentleman and kind to me and my children."

"Leon told Anna that it was a pleasure to get to know her and her sweet children and that her husband was a lucky man to have her as his wife."

"Leon, I have to ask you a serious question."

Anna took a deep breath and blurted out the truth. "Recently, I found out that my husband is a bigamist! He's been convicted for marrying another woman illegally and is in prison in another state. Leon, my parents are wealthy and constantly worry about any kind of gossip about our family. They'll disown me if they find out about him. As soon as this house is finished, I am getting my marriage secretly annulled. Then, I'm going to pack up, take my children and leave Canada, and move to Texas in the United States where I'm going to start a new life."

"Abigail, at first I was shocked when she told me about her husband. Then, Anna asked me if I'd ever fallen in love before, and I told her no. Then, she asked a question I'll never forget. 'Leon, will you marry me? Please don't answer me yet until I explain why.' She told me she wanted to give her children a respectable name. Then, I told her the truth: 'Anna, I'm not in love with you.'

"She pleaded with me, stressing that she didn't want to live with me and that no money would ever exchange hands—no support for the children would be necessary. 'It's why I plan to move to Texas where no one would ever find us,' she said.

"I didn't know what to do at first, but then I had second thoughts. I thought about it for several days and knew it was the act of a desperate mother afraid of ruining her family's reputation, and then I wondered what would happen if I ever did fall in love and wanted to get married? Would my love be able to accept what I did for friendship and concern for another man's children? What would I do if I were in her shoes? I really didn't know how a woman thinks or feels, but in the end, I couldn't refuse her desperate attempt to start a new life. It's the only reason I married Anna.

"I'm so sorry, my love. Can you still love me? Leon pleaded, Can you trust me and wait to marry me someday? I promise to be faithful until death do us part."

"Leon, I love you more for what you did for Anna and her children. You are a good, kind man, and I'll love you forever."

Little by little, Abigail and Leon shared plans for a lifetime together when the time would be right. They also kept their love affair private. Abigail knew she couldn't tell her father or mother because she knew they would stop her from going to the park and she would never see Leon again.

The unexpected happened when twenty-five-year-old Abigail found out she was expecting Leon's baby. Her father yelled, slapped her hard across the face, and told her she had to get out of the house as soon as possible. Having an unwed, pregnant daughter was a disgrace. Her father gave her a small amount of cash and told her he never wanted to see her again. Her mother cried, and Abigail promised to keep in touch with her. I was shocked to hear how her parents treated her. I wondered why. She was family. Even though I don't officially have one, it boggles my mind how cruel her father was and her mother had no say in the matter.

Leon swore he would take care of Abigail and their baby and buy her an apartment building right over the border on the West Side of Buffalo, New York. By befriending Edward Pickett, Leon turned his plans into reality, especially when he became my builder. While Leon built me for Abigail, he also helped Abigail and their child settle into an apartment next door, almost right next to me. Leon continued to travel back and forth to Canada, gradually completing his building projects before planning to move to the United States to permanently be with his Abigail and little boy Edward.

For the first three years of my life, Abigail and her young son lived alone with occasional visits from Leon, but everything changed one day when Leon moved into Abigail's apartment as a boarder. I couldn't help but notice how in love they were. He cared for their little boy nicknamed Eddie. Leon constantly played and read books to him and would take him for walks on Potomac Avenue. He even bought him a little red wagon to pull, which he filled with his favorite toys. I wished I was human. Then, maybe I could have a son of my own someday.

A year after Leon moved in, they lived as a united couple, saving their money and making plans to get married when the time was right. They still wanted to buy a home of their own, and Leon wanted to buy his own gas station on the West Side. It was also during this time that they both became American citizens. It was a happy time for both of them. It was the same year that Abigail sold me to Carrie Detrick for $11,200.

Yearly, Leon received a detailed letter from his legal wife Anna in Texas. In it, he would receive a thank you for his commitment to her and her children, along with an update about their lives. He would answer her letter and tell her about his love for Abigail—the real love of his life.

It was good to find out that Anna had a wonderful life in Texas and was operating a small orphanage out of her large home. Her younger sister moved to Texas and into her home to help her take care of the children while she worked. She also promised to raise them if anything ever happened to her and, if possible, continue to manage the orphanage.

On July 15, 1907, Leon received a large envelope containing a death notice from his wife's sister Bella and a copy of Anna's will. She also wrote that her beloved sister had died peacefully a week earlier.

Anna's orphanage was named Leon Edward O'Shannon's Haven for Orphan Children. Bella's letter also expressed how grateful Anna was and how much she valued Leon's friendship and sacrifice.

When he received the news about Anna's death, Leon was emotional and sad. It was the end of a friendship and the beginning of his new life. Abigail had compassion for the woman she never met and respected. They both had something in common because they both had to keep secrets. I realized that all women knew that being unmarried with a child was unacceptable in society. Only once did Abigail have contact with her own mother, and it was right before she moved to the United States. After that, all letters were returned. She often cried muffled tears in the middle of the night while Eddie slept. I wish I could have comforted her, but all I could do was keep her in my thoughts.

Abigail and Leon's love had multiple obstacles; only now there would be no more secrets. Leon's dedication to her and his secret son was a gift of love between the three of them.

During the four years that Abigail and Leon lived in my building, they became close friends with Jenny Etta and Millie. They were the first people Abigail told when Leon received the news about Anna's passing. One was a sixty-three-year-old French widow named Jenny Etta Marcotte who moved into the other second-floor apartment. She was tall, regal, and wore her hair pulled back in a silvery gray bun. She had no children of her own, but little Edward adored her, and she loved him back. The other woman, Millie, was a fifty-year-old German spinster whose mother died of cholera in 1854 when Millie was four years old. . Listening to all of them speak to each other on a daily basis gave me a bird's eye view of a love story I'll never forget.

Tears streamed down Abigail's cheeks when she shared her story. Her friends expressed their happiness for both of them, showing joy with warm hugs and tears of their own. Leon and Abigail were married a week after receiving Anna's death notice.

Within a brief period of time, when Abigail and Leon bought a small house just three doors away from me on Potomac Avenue in 1908, Leon purchased a neighborhood gas station only blocks away from their new home, and I would often see Abigail passing by with Edward, pulling his wagon. He was growing into an energetic young boy, and I enjoyed watching him play catch and tag in the street almost every day after school. Abigail would visit Jenny Etta and Millie every week, and I was grateful to still see her and hear about their lives.

My first tenants turned their dreams into reality, overcoming many challenges and obstacles along the way. They were brave and never gave up on their future. I'm determined to be a trailblazer too.

. . . .

CHAPTER THREE

Memories and Tales from the Past

J enny Etta lived in my building for an additional ten years after Abigail and Leon moved down the street. Unfortunately, at the age of seventy-two, she was hospitalized with influenza and never made it home again.

Jenny Etta was a sixty-three-year-old widow when she moved into the apartment right across Abigail's. Her husband, Daniel, was a locomotive engineer on the New York Central Railroad. He died suddenly of a heart attack in 1894, when he was sixty-seven. It happened one morning just before he started up his train. Jenny was devastated because Daniel was the love of her life. After his death, she moved her frail, elderly mother into her small home on Bristol Street in Buffalo. How I missed Jenny Etta and her memorable tales of her mom. But what I remember most was that they both survived a tragic fire that was near their home.

It happened on July 14, 1895; the famous Niagara Starch Works Factory exploded on Howard Street only a couple of blocks away from their Bristol Street home. It was the scene of a horrible large boiler explosion. Many people were killed or injured, including eleven young children. Jenny's little house shook, and two of her windows broke from the debris that landed in front of her house.

Jenny and her mother heard the screams of frightened residents and bystanders. Both women were scared and huddled together praying for the victims—and for themselves.

Then, in the fall of 1899, Jenny's mother died in her sleep. Shortly after the loss of her mother, she decided to move into my building. I remember Jenny saying repeatedly how lucky she was to live here. My building provided Jenny with valuable friendships. But I wish I could've let her know that I was a friend too. Jenny Etta never wanted to be alone, and thanks to Abigail and Eddie, she never was. She loved little Eddie and cared for him when Abigail shopped for groceries or had errands to run. When Jenny had time, she loved to walk through the neighborhood with her little boy, talking to everyone they'd meet.

Abigail loved to listen to Jenny's exciting stories—and so did I! Her life was full of adventure and change. I've been standing here on solid ground for all my life living through my tenants' lives. One morning when Abigail and Jenny were having coffee together, she told her about one of the most exciting moments of her life. It happened on Saturday, February 16, 1861, when Jenny Etta and Daniel watched as Abraham Lincoln's inaugural train stopped in Buffalo on his way to accept the presidency of the United States, and Mr. Lincoln was greeted by former President Millard Fillmore and ten thousand local supporters.

Mural of Abraham Lincoln speaking from the balcony of the American Hotel on February 16, 1861. The mural is on the second floor of The Buffalo History Museum. Left to right: Almon M. Clapp, A. Bemis, Abraham Lincoln, Millard Fillmore, and Gen. Daniel Bidwell. Collection of The Buffalo History Museum. TBHM photo collection, Picture. T43, Series 1, Box 5, Folder 3.

"We were two of thousands of people lined up on Main Street hoping to see him and hear his speech. We saw the artillery brigade and their salute to Mr. Lincoln. It was one of the most exhilarating moments of my life. We stood as close as we could to the American Hotel on Main Street. There were people everywhere, and all the ladies waved their handkerchiefs in the air. Every building was decorated with flags and banners. There was hope in the air—even though we were on the brink of war." Jenny said. I couldn't help but smile at the memory. She witnessed one of the most important events in American history.

Jenny explained that the incoming Republican President Lincoln had pledged to keep slavery out of the territories, but seven slave states soon succeeded and formed a new nation called the Confederate States of America. It triggered a declaration of war on April 12, 1861, and full-scale fighting began in 1862.

Four years later, on April 14, 1865, President Abraham Lincoln was assassinated by John Wilkes Booth at the Ford's Theatre in Washington, D.C. His funeral train arrived in Buffalo at 7:00 a.m. on April 27, 1865, at the same Exchange Street Station he had arrived at four years earlier on his way to Washington.

City Hotel at Exchange and Michigan Streets. The view is from April of 1865 when the hotel was draped in mourning for Abraham Lincoln. Collection of The Buffalo History Museum. General photograph collection, Buildings – Residences – Hotels.

"When I think about it," Jenny said, "I feel the same way I felt when I witnessed the sadness and loss of a great president. It was a privilege to be part of the thousands of people who viewed his open coffin. It's a sight I'll never forget."

Jenny's childhood growing up in Auburn, New York, took us back in time, and we looked forward to hearing more stories. Another remarkable story was about her closest childhood friend, Annie Edson Taylor. She explained that Annie's father owned a local flour mill and would often give Jenny's family extra flour. He also took both girls on long carriage rides in the country on Sunday afternoons. When I heard her talk, I could visualize in my mind's eye what it must have been like. Boy, I felt like I was there with both the girls having fun in the sun.

Annie kept in touch with Jenny at least once a year even after she married and became a school teacher. Only when her husband was killed in what he called The War to Make Men Free did Annie decide to make a real name for herself.

On October 24, 1901, sixty-three-year-old Annie became the first person to survive a trip over Niagara Falls. As soon as Jenny Etta found out, she told everyone who would listen how excited she was for her friend. "She did it! My best friend, Annie, took the ride with her cat in a padded pickle barrel. Then, a boat towed Annie to the falls and dropped her into the rapids in the Niagara River above the 170 foot Canadian Falls. It took her less than twenty minutes to go over the Falls, only she had to stay in the barrel a lot longer before she was rescued. She was lucky because her only injury was a cut on her head when she got out of the barrel!"

Abigail's other confidante and friend, Millie Schmidt, who lived a floor above in one of my third-floor apartments had a canary named Buddy. I loved hearing his beautiful songs throughout the day. Buddy was the star of the building, and his fan club was my tenants and especially me.

Whenever I think of Millie, I am reminded of what happened to her mom when she was only four years old. She died of cholera, a terrible epidemic in 1854. After her mother's death, her mother's sister Greta and her husband William moved in with Millie and her father George.

Millie's family originally arrived in Buffalo in the 1800s with several thousand other mostly skilled German immigrants. Her father became a successful shoemaker with a small shop on the West Side. Her aunt and uncle continued to help him raise her until she graduated from high school.

When she was twenty-five, Millie was one of hundreds of volunteers who served a Thanksgiving dinner to one-hundred eighty news and bootblack boys. She was shocked by their young ages. I thought they were as young as six or seven and into their teens. She told Abigail and Anna that she would never forget the sight of the young children. They could work for up to sixty-six hours per week selling newspapers and shining shoes because their families were dependent on their wages for survival. When I heard about this, I couldn't believe it. Mainly because I've never met a little boy except for Abigail's son Eddie. I would have loved to have a family of my own and a young son. Wishful thinking was all I could do. There is no sense in dwelling on what I'll never have.

Millie told the woman that some of the boys were runaways or that they were sent out to live on the streets because their families couldn't or wouldn't take care of them. When the Buffalo Children's Aid Society was founded in 1873, Millie decided she would dedicate her life to helping all the news and bootblack boys she could. That same year, Millie's father died and left her a significant inheritance, which allowed her to give a loving home to a homeless child. When I heard Millie's mission in life, I began to learn what it's like to be human. I've already learned how each of my tenants was unique. Not one person is the same. Rather, they are one of a kind.

The following year, Millie was hired as a secretary for the society and helped plan and prepare for the second massive Thanksgiving dinner for over a thousand boys at the Seventy-Fourth Regiment

Armory. She wanted to take each child home and save them all, but all she could do at the time was to make sure they each received a special dinner.

Millie told us about a little boy named Teddy. He was only eight years old and lived alone on the streets.

"Me mum died," he told Millie. "Me pop drank, hit me, and told me to get out and get me a new home. Me friends helped me get a newsboy job. They told me they'd watch out for me."

It was when Millie invited Teddy to her home for supper that he said, "I don't need help, lady. I take care of meself."

Millie immediately held out her hand and he took it.

It wasn't long before Teddy was living with Millie, attending school, and being a good student. Tragedy struck when Teddy died at the age of ten. He was killed in a terrible carriage accident while walking home from school when he darted out into the street. Millie was heartbroken when her little Irishman passed away. When she first received the news, she stood in the middle of her kitchen floor stunned. A moment later, with tears flowing, she ran into Teddy's bedroom, threw herself on his bed, clutched his pillow and sobbed. I wanted to comfort her, but I couldn't. It's a dilemma I have to live with. Hearing my tenants' stories made me feel like I was a part of their everyday lives. It's another reason why I have to share them with you, my reader.

Hours later, she left his bed to go to the bathroom. She washed her face with cold water and hoped that she woke up from a horrible dream. Only it wasn't a dream; it was the beginning of a nightmare and an empty life without the lovable little boy.

Teddy was befriended from the very beginning by another bootblack boy named William, who was several years older than him, and Millie had often invited him to come over for Sunday dinners. William was a good-looking, cheerful young man, and when Teddy died, he was as heartbroken as Millie.

A year later, Millie took William into her home permanently. Several months later, she asked him if she could adopt him. He cried, hugged her, and said he would be proud to have her for his mom. Then, she helped William get a job as a laborer on a construction site, and two years later, he was hired as an apprentice carpenter. He lived with Millie for five years until he married at the age of twenty-one.

William loved having Millie for a mother, and she loved him back. His own mother had kicked him out of the house when he was only twelve and was forced to leave his younger brothers and sisters behind. His mother told him he was old enough to fend for himself. William was devoted to Millie. Once he became a grown man with a family of his own, he eagerly picked her up every weekend and took her home with him to spend time with her two granddaughters and his wife. She baked cookies and cakes for the children, played house with them, read them storybooks, and talked about Teddy and how special he was.

Millie loved living in my building, and I loved having her here. I would have liked to have her for a mother. I now realize how much I want to be human. But the next best thing is to have free will and think like all the tenants who inspire me to treasure life itself. Millie was here for eight more years until she died suddenly of influenza in the middle of the night. It's awful when we lose the people we love. I'm only a building without a heartbeat, yet I love my tenants. I grieve for all of them when they pass away.

During Jenny Etta's and Millie's time in my building, there were other tenants I want to tell you about. In fact, all my tenants helped me cope with life, but four of them even helped to build me. There were two Irishmen, an Italian, and a German. Each of them knew Abigail because she talked to them every day while I was being built. They would greet little Eddie and spend a minute or two trying to make him smile.

James and Johnnie Fitzpatrick, my Irish brothers, lived in one of my fourth-floor apartments. Both men were seasoned grain scoopers from the First Ward in the South Buffalo-Seneca Street area, home to mainly unskilled and skilled laborer immigrants, mostly from Ireland. The Irish moved there because it was close to the Buffalo Union Furnace, railroads, and massive grain elevators on Buffalo's waterfront. Both brothers participated in the Great Strike of 1899, which wasn't against the shipping companies or industrialists but against the freight contractors. When they were hired to work on my apartment building as laborers by an independent contractor, they were lucky to be working because the Fitzpatrick brothers were blacklisted. It happened when they went on strike, and both men realized that they would never be allowed to work in the elevators again. Actually, it was the Irish saloon owners in the First Ward who held the contracts with the elevator and shipping companies to control labor suppliers, and they were unforgiving.

In 1901, both brothers, now in their twenties, attended the Irish football match at the Pan-American Exposition. They came home with cuts, bruises, black eyes, and lots of tales they loved to tell. Then, two weeks after I was completed, they moved into my building and were immediately hired at the Richmond Mantel Company on Niagara Street to work in the cabinet room. Then, in 1907, six years later, they both became firemen for the city of Buffalo. Later, the brothers were hired and worked together at the Hook and Ladder #1 on South Park Avenue and Whitfield Street. It was quite a distance from me, and I missed them even though they only lived in their apartment for a month. Whenever they were in the building, there was some excitement because they were full of life and played jokes on each other all the time, and I loved it.

Then, there was Giuseppe Benevento, an immigrant, who was from the province of Palermo, Sicily. He lived on the third floor, and he worked as my skilled laborer during my construction. He was saving money to bring his young family to America. When he moved into my building, he had been recently hired as a night watchman at King Spring Company on Niagara Street. It was a good, steady job and soon he would be able to save enough money to send for his family.

Giuseppe was grateful and proud to be in America. He even bought a medium-sized American flag and made a special stand for it in his living room. I watched him pray every night and then gently touch that flag.

I heard him talk about his family all the time, telling everyone how America saved him. In Sicily, he was a poor farmer struggling to survive. His family suffered from terrible rural poverty and political and economic hardships. When he first arrived in America, he was able to get a job as a skilled laborer because of the carpentry skills his father taught him growing up.

Giuseppe had another special skill he learned in Sicily. His wine making ability was appreciated by all the tenants, especially at Christmas time. They would wait patiently for their homemade bottle of red Sicilian wine. I wanted a bottle too. I had to laugh at myself. I couldn't drink it anyway, but I could smell its delicious flavor and pretend I did! Giuseppe, with help from his friend from church, would prepare his small kitchen for the annual labor of love. When the wine was finally ready, he would walk from apartment to apartment delivering his special gift. Everyone would smile, hug him, and wish him Merry Christmas.

During the next decade, Giuseppe saved enough money to buy a two-family house on Potomac, just down the street from me. It was when he was able to pay for his wife's and two daughters' steerage to America. He was also able to bring his recently widowed sister and her grown-up daughter to live with them. I was happy for him and his family.

When Giuseppe left my building, his tenant friends gave him a big surprise going away party. He didn't know it, but I was there celebrating too. It was still hard letting go of the people I loved. Only I knew I was their transitional home on the way to their hopes and dreams.

Fredrick Bayer also lived in my building and was good friends with Giuseppe. He was a twenty-six-year-old concrete apprentice who was tall and soft-spoken. His great-great-grandfather was among the first wave of German immigrants who came after the European Revolution of 1848 with the German States. His grandpa was one of the forty-eighters, the rebels who fought for the unification for the German people, and he was one of thousands of political refugees who fled to the United States and ended up in Buffalo's Kaisertown—a neighborhood that surrounded Clinton Street and was enclosed by the Buffalo River. It's where generations of his family settled and where Fredrick grew up.

Fredrick started to court Marie, Giuseppe's twenty-three-year-old niece shortly after she came with her uncle to visit him. Marie was dark-haired and very pretty. Right away, I saw that they were attracted to each other. She was learning English, and Fredrick offered to help tutor her on the weekends. She agreed, and it was the beginning of their official courtship that led to their marriage within a year.

Fredrick and Marie lived in my building an additional year before they were able to buy their own small home on the West Side.

Last, but not least, was the legendary Mr. Speziali's grocery store. This deli was on my first floor with an apartment in the back. It's where his family lived. The deli was extremely popular in the neighborhood and always busy. They sold canned goods, meats, fruit, vegetables, and ice cream. Boy, was I lucky I could smell all his fresh vegetables and see his baskets of apples, round wheels of parmesan and provolone cheese, mixed with salami, bologna, and ham. Then, there was a large pickle barrel filled to the brim with dill pickles with fresh dill floating on top and its wooden handle with holes in it to drain them. If I could have only tasted them, my lips would have puckered up like my tenants' who loved them. Every week, I saw a neighbor's German shepherd, named Prince, who became famous among my tenants and the neighborhood. The dog's owner, a local plumbing and heating contractor named John Henry, would send him over to Speziali's almost every day where he'd bark at the screen door in the summer and scratch at the door in the winter until someone let him in. In his mouth, Prince held a little brown bag with a note and some money. Mr. Speziali would open the bag and read the note. Then, he'd put the order in a brown paper bag with the change—but only after Prince was given his vanilla ice-cream cone. The dog would lay down and hold it in his paws licking it until it was gone! Mr. Speziali then put the bag back in Prince's mouth, and he would head home wagging his tail.

The Speziali's were in my building for ten more years until they moved to open a larger store on Grant Street. I won't forget the wonderful scents from the deli, and I can still smell them in my mind.

CHAPTER FOUR

· · · · · · · · · · · · · · · ·

Buffalo's Young Suffragettes

My tenants have been memorable, including my Irish identical twins Patricia and Kathleen Duffy. The twins had confidence, spunk, and firsthand knowledge of what their immigrant parents and grandparents had achieved. They both begged, pleaded, and tried to convince their parents, Maureen and Danny, to let them live in my building while attending D'Youville College, located walking distance away. The college was founded by the Grey Nuns and was only the second women's college built in New York State in 1908. Finally, their parents relented and let them rent one of my two fourth-floor apartments.

Their parents' families arrived in Buffalo together from Kilkelly, Ireland, in 1861, the same year the Civil War started. They came to America with thousands of others because of Ireland's terrible Potato Crop Famine, hoping that America would be the answer to their prayers.

Arriving via the Erie Canal, both families lived east of Buffalo and were among the second wave of Irish immigrants to arrive here. Their shanty village was isolated by railroad tracks and was eventually known as the Valley. Later, the entire area became the location of the first animal stockyards in the city. Both couples had limited resources and skills, and an inability to speak English.

In Ireland, both families were best friends. They had lived in thatched huts without electricity, surviving by hard work on farmland owned by the English. If they'd stayed in Ireland, they knew they would have died.

Tommy and Frances Duffy, and Bill and Sarah Murphy were overwhelmed at first, but it wasn't long before Tommy and Bill got jobs digging ditches on the Erie Canal. Their wives worked as charwomen for as long as possible before having their babies only a month apart. A grandma in their overcrowded tenement house on Seneca Street helped deliver a girl named Maureen to Frances Duffy and a boy named Danny to Sarah Murphy. Each woman left her cleaning job and cared for other people's children while nursing their own babies. The conditions in the tenement were deplorable and unsanitary, and they dreamt of moving to a safer place as soon as they could afford a place together in a modest rooming house.

I listened to Kathleen and Patricia tell their friends how difficult it was for their parents and grandparents to survive in America. I can't imagine what it was like for them, and their stories made me grateful that I'm a clean, cared for building.

I have to mention that Frances Duffy had two stillborn babies before arriving in America, and Sarah Murphy experienced a miscarriage a year before Danny was born. When both children were young, they played, argued sometimes, and had fun together. Growing up, Danny delivered newspapers before and after school, and Maureen helped her mother mend clothes for others in the evenings.

When they were teenagers, they went their separate ways; only everything changed in 1893 when Danny's father, Bill Murphy, tripped and fell into a ditch at work and died of a broken neck. The Duffy family did everything they could to help support Danny and his mother Sarah and spent time with them every day. It's then that Maureen and Danny renewed their friendship and developed feelings for each other.

A year later, Danny's mum, Sarah, became very sick and died of heart failure. Frances vowed to keep her memory alive by making her favorite dinner once a week, invite Danny over, and help him out financially whenever they could. Dinners together were a time to share their memories of both Danny's parents, especially on holidays. Frances would light a candle for Sarah at church every week and missed her friend desperately.

She cooked, cleaned, and became a seamstress for families who lived on the other side of the city. Maureen and Danny continued to get closer and declared their love for each other. They were engaged in 1884, and it wasn't long before they were able to afford to rent two rooms in a modest rooming house where they could live together. It's then that they decided not to take their wedding vows until they could save enough money to make a down payment on a home of their own in a safe neighborhood on the growing West Side of Buffalo where jobs were plentiful.

Six years later, in 1890, Maureen and Danny were married by a justice of the peace immediately after Maureen discovered she was pregnant. Fortunately, they saved enough money to afford a modest home on Connecticut Street and moved in right before the birth of their twins. Maureen's parents also moved into a small cottage apartment only a couple doors away. Growing up, the twins and their parents made sure that Grandpa Tommy and Frances Duffy had everything they needed, including a family dinner on Sunday afternoons. When the twins were little, they spent most of their time with their grandparents while their mother and father were at work.

The Duffy and Murphy family history was an eye-opener. All I thought about was the strength and courage both families had while seeking a better life in America.

Patricia and Kathleen's parents and grandparents never ever let them forget their immigrant roots. I found out that when they were little, Grandma Frances would tell them to be proud and independent. "We Irish have always been controlled," she'd say. "I want you to have the freedom we never had. Work hard, get an education, and earn your wings so you can fly on your own."

"Grandma, we'll fly for you. We promise. You wait and see" said the twins.

In 1908, Grandma Frances unexpectedly died at the age of seventy-one. Their Grandpa Duffy continued to try to live alone, but his legs were giving out, and he needed help. The girls begged him to come live with them. Initially, he fought the idea but eventually agreed and moved in with the Duffy family.

The girls said that Grandpa Duffy often spoke about a popular song written in 1863. Most likely it was English and was created by John J. Poole a year earlier, but it was called "No Irish Need Apply," and there were two versions. Men would sing it one way, and then little ten-year-old Kitty O'Neil would sing her own version.

"I knew her family back home in Ireland before they moved to America where Kitty was born," Grandpa Duffy said smiling. "She grew up to be a famous New York-based singer and jig dancer."

"Grandpa, what happened to Kitty?" Kathleen said.

"Well, she ended up supporting herself, her family, and a variety of other people who took advantage of her innocence. I don't want you both to be famous like Kitty. I want you both to make a proud history for yourselves and your future children."

Their Grandpa constantly talked with the girls about what was happening in America and abroad. "Please get the right to vote before I die," he'd say over and over. "I pray that God will let me live long enough to see me angels vote."

Whenever the twins went home to visit their parents for their weekly Sunday dinners, they feasted on meals of pot roast or roast beef and mashed potatoes. They loved their Momma's cabbage, boiled potatoes, and ham. Sometimes they had carrots, corn, peas, homemade bread, buttermilk biscuits, oatmeal cookies, and chocolate cake. Usually, they took the leftovers home to eat during the week, and I'd watch them enjoy each meal and longed to eat with them too. Living on the West Side in their small, neat, vertical house made it possible for the twins' parents to give Patricia and Kathleen an excellent education and the opportunity to earn a college degree. Their father Danny worked as a Buffalo Police lieutenant, and Maureen was an elementary school teacher—both respectable occupations for first-generation Irish Americans. When the girls applied and were accepted into D'Youville College, the Duffys were proud of themselves and their daughters. Grandpa Duffy bought Patricia and Kathleen each a red rose in memory of Grandma Frances. I know she would have been proud of her granddaughters. They were a proud Irish family who honored the struggles of the past.

On their first day of college classes, the girls were befriended by a sophomore named Bridget Murphy. Bridget was a vibrant, curly-haired redhead suffragette. "I'm as Irish as Patty's Pig," she'd say, and the twins couldn't stop laughing.

Bridget liked the twins' energy, and they connected immediately. Eventually, the girls invited Bridget over to their apartment to hold her monthly suffragette meetings. At that time, most of their college peers were conservative, and only a few were openly supportive of a woman's right to vote. This was all new to me, and I carefully listened to all their conversations regarding the Suffragettes.

I saw them squeeze eight young women into their tiny apartment. They sat on chairs, on the floor, and a few even brought their own small wooden crates to sit on. They wanted the right to vote and vowed to work hard to get it. They discussed the need for economic, political, and social reforms and challenged the traditional roles of women.

I had an extensive history lesson when the twins found out that Jane Addams and her friend, Ellen Gates Star, pioneer social workers and reformers, cofounded the foundling settlement houses like the Hull Settlement House on the West Side of Chicago, Illinois, in response to growing poverty, with a goal of getting the rich and poor in society to live more closely together in an interdependent community. The women were advocates for fair child labor laws, women's suffrage, and immigration policies. In 1889, Jane Addams was named cowinner of the Nobel Peace Prize.

It was then that all three girls decided to spend the summer in Chicago in 1912, volunteering to help at the Hull House. If they could get there on their own, they would be able to have free room and board in exchange for working to help the nonprofit serve the inner-city neighborhood, especially the immigrant population.

Patricia and Kathleen's parents said yes and paid their rent on my apartment for the entire summer as well as their fare both ways to Chicago. Bridget's family also paid for her trip too. Both sets of parents felt it was an investment in their futures. The girls promised their suffragette friends who couldn't afford to go that when they got home, they would share everything they learned with them.

When they first arrived at Hull House, the girls were overwhelmed when they saw how difficult it was for new immigrants to adjust to life in America. Most came with no understanding of this country's culture and spoke only their native language. Bridget, Kathleen, and Patricia had extensive conversations late into the night about how the immigrant families had the strength of steel in the face of poverty and discrimination. They each vowed to never forget how good it felt to help mothers and children learn to read and write and adapt to an American way of life.

When they came home from Chicago, they were all determined to work harder to advance the suffrage movement. During their meetings, I overheard discussions regarding their plans to march in the first Suffrage Parade on March 3, 1913, in Washington, District of Columbia, organized by Alice Paul and Lucy Burns, American suffragettes. Kathleen, Patricia, Bridget, and their friends organized a bus trip to New York City to meet up with the New York City delegation and travel together to the parade route.

They were honored to ride behind Elizabeth Freeman of the New York State Suffrage Association, with her horse and carriage leading the way to Washington. My young suffragettes wanted the right to vote and to have a voice like men did. I didn't think that they were asking for too much. I was shocked to learn that women were treated as less than men, and I couldn't comprehend why. I would have marched with them if I could. I know I'm a male, but I'm learning what women of all ages had to deal with. I'm in a unique situation. I get to see life from a woman's perspective, and by the time my tales are told, you'll find out how having a man's and a woman's perspective made me stronger.

My young suffragettes considered themselves modern women in a struggle for their right to vote. I constantly heard them talk about how Kathleen, Patricia, Bridget, and their friends wore one of the first modern brassieres. It was created by Mary Phelps Jacob, a young New York socialite who was frustrated with her corset and wanted to keep the support rods from sticking out from underneath her evening gown. All the girls wore modern brassieres on their march to Washington, D.C., on March 3, 1913.

It wasn't long after the first marchers arrived when something terrible had happened. Hundreds and thousands of people, mostly men, were already in Washington to celebrate Woodrow Wilson's presidential inauguration scheduled for the following day. Five thousand women were in Washington to demand the right to vote under the leadership of Alice Paul. Then suddenly, men were breaking up the parade, and many of the marchers were beaten, shoved, and hurt by the angry mob.

Bridget, Kathleen, and Patricia missed the riot because while they were getting ready to march along the parade route, they heard the terrible news and how it had fractured the entire parade. They were overwhelmed, shocked, and scared for the suffragettes at the front of the parade. When reality set in, they were more determined than ever to continue fighting for a woman's right to vote.

I was happy the twins and Bridget made it home safely. I listened while they talked to each other about another major problem that happened on the day of the Washington parade. Anna Julie Cooper, a Black suffragette and leader of the Alfa Suffrage Club, asked the organizers of the parade if she and her members could walk alongside the other women leaders, but she was refused and was told that they could walk instead at the end of the parade. They were angry and upset that suffragettes would be unjust and treat another member disrespectfully.

When the parade moved on, a brave woman named Ida B. Wells Barnett joined the White Illinois delegation, marching between two White supporters. "We must include all women, or we will never be free," Ida stated, and the Alfa Suffrage Club was then allowed to march along with her. When the girls came home, all they could talk about was the courage of Anna Julie Cooper and Ida B. Wells Barnett.

Both women were born slaves in Cooper, North Carolina, in 1858. They were crusaders for justice and believed that only through political activity and empowerment would African women have freedom and equal rights. That's why their being accepted into the Suffrage Parade on that day was so important.

During this time, I found out that the suffrage movement in this country began on July 19, 1848, when the first women's rights convention was held in Seneca Falls, New York. It was there that Susan B. Anthony spoke to a crowd of over two hundred women and forty men. Her famous quote "failure is impossible" motivated them to work harder. On the second day of the convention, Abolitionist Frederick Douglas delivered an impressive speech that brought the suffrage movement and the abolition movement against slavery together.

On August 7, 1913, Theodore Roosevelt's Progressive Party became the first national party to adopt a women's suffrage plank under their equal suffrage statement. The party met in 1912 when Theodore Roosevelt lost the presidential nomination of the Republican Party to incumbent President William Taft. The party was called the Bull Moose Party, and the members were college-educated men and women that believed the government could be a tool for change. Jane Addams supported the party and said, "The Progressive Party, believing that no people can justly claim to be a true democracy, which denies political rights on account of sex, pledges itself to the task of securing equal suffrage to men and women alike."

Patricia and Kathleen gave me history lessons I'll never forget. I found out that there was an important connection between Toynbee Hall in London, England, and the suffrage movement in America because of their mutual goals to bridge the gap between people of all social and financial levels and help others less fortunate and to have a future without poverty.

I'm proud of the help I was able to give these girls. They didn't realize it, but I supported their cause and wanted equality for them and all women. I was glad to be their safe haven—a place where they could talk freely, without fear.

Bridget attended the twins' graduation on a warm spring day in June of 1914. The Duffys had a small graduation party in their home for their daughters and their suffragette friends were all invited. It was a day filled with hope for the future, and the girls promised Grandpa Duffy that women would get the right to vote and that he would witness it in his lifetime.

Two weeks later, though, their lives changed forever. Bridget died suddenly in a drowning accident during a family picnic at the lake. Her family tried to save her, but it was too late. Kathleen and Patricia were devastated. Their best friend was gone. They kept asking each other, "Why? Why did this have to happen? She was our hero." I listened and felt their loss, too. Bridget was their role model and leader of their suffrage group. All they could do was cry and pray for the strength to handle her death. Although they found a little comfort in spending time with Bridget's parents, their hearts were broken and filled with grief.

I've learned how grief has many layers. When it first happened, everyone crowded into Kathleen and Patricia's apartment at various times and, honestly, it was overwhelming to witness. Initially, the twins were shocked and couldn't stop crying, but then as time passed, they described the pain as feeling empty inside, and I noticed that they would sometimes become angry.

I heard Kathleen and Patricia crying night after night for weeks at a time, but when the tears subsided, they vowed to take over Bridget's leadership role in the local suffrage movement and worked harder than ever to honor her memory. They even spoke to Bridget's spirit, and it appeared to give them comfort.

On June 9, 1914, both girls played major roles in planning and supporting a Western New York Suffrage Parade down Main Street in the city of Buffalo. The women leaders, including the twins, carried flags and banners. They were accompanied by little girls and older women suffragettes in carriages. What a sight it must have been. All the suffragettes wore white dresses and three-cornered colonial hats. Twenty-five thousand suffragettes and supporters marched in that parade. The city even provided a police escort to lead the march, and 150 policemen walked the parade route with them.

THE WOMAN SUFFRAGE PARADE IN JUNE: AT NIAGARA SQUARE

Suffrage Parade in Niagara Square, 1914.
Collection of The Buffalo History Museum.
General photograph collection, Political Movements.

Afterward, when the twins were back in my apartment, I heard Patricia saying that they even had a group of forty-five men carrying banners. The men were led by Chauncey J. Hamlin, a lawyer from a prominent Buffalo family.

The girls knew that Bridget would have been proud of what they'd done. She'd given them the strength to keep fighting, and they knew that she'd marched along beside them.

Their march made the national news because it was peaceful and supported by thousands of people. The *New York Times* declared in October 1915 that the Western New York suffragettes had made remarkable progress. The twins knew that Bridget smiled down on them and urged them not to quit until all women were granted the right to vote.

CHAPTER FIVE

The Suffragettes Grow Up:
Love, Loss, and World War I

K athleen and Patricia became fast friends with Suffragette Janet Fortherington, a Buffalo teacher of physical culture, and attended some of her meetings. Her influence on the twins was strong. On July 14, 1917, Janet was among the first suffragettes to picket and chain themselves to Washington, D.C., monuments. Doctors, nurses, students, and teachers all participated. Mothers and grandmothers also picketed, and many women were arrested—they ranged in age from seventeen to seventy.

Those arrested were fined $25 and sent to jail if they couldn't pay. Janet was sent to the Occoquan Workhouse located in Fairfax County, Virginia, for sixty days. One night forty guards attacked the group, beating many and sending some to the hospital with serious injuries. The group's sentence—including Miss Fortherington's— was reduced to three days. Luckily, Janet was not one of the women beaten by the guards. The publicity the attack received proved to be important for the movement and won them many new supporters, both men and women.

The twins' apartment had a poster on their wall that was remarkable. It was created by Buffalo artist Evelyn Rumsey Cary.

Its message read: "Give her the fruit of her hand and let her own works praise her in the gates."

The poster featured a woman dressed in a flowing white gown transforming into a tree, and the arms are extensions bearing fruit. I know how inspired they were by the poster because the woman was in front of a building that resembled the white house. Often the twins talked about how it reinforced the beliefs of the suffrage movement and a woman's civil rights. Time was changing rapidly, and our country needed help. The war in Europe was underway, and our government asked all women nationwide to turn in their corsets for the iron rods they contained. The twins, their friends, and women all over the country collected thousands of corsets for the cause. In the end, women donated twenty-eight thousand tons of metal with enough to build two battleships.

On May 17, 1917, the Selective Service Act passed and took effect immediately. The twins were upset because all the young men they knew were going to be drafted into the war within three separate registrations. The last registration was held on September 12, 1918, for men eighteen to forty-five years of age. If I would have been capable, I would have stopped the war and wondered why no one did.

During this time, the suffragette meetings in the girls' apartment turned to helping the war effort and providing support to local families and children while their husbands, fathers, and sons went off to war. Several nights a week, the girls volunteered to help organize massive supplies of food and medical supplies to be sent overseas by the American Red Cross.

By the time of the last draft, Patricia and Kathleen both cried constantly, and I couldn't do anything to comfort them, especially when their good friends Patrick Kelly and Shawn Hennessey enlisted in the army.

When they came over to pick up the twins and take them to an early movie on the weekends, they would invite them both to their weekly Sunday dinner. The war in Europe was in full force, and the girls were constantly worried and kept as busy as possible volunteering to help the war effort. Soon the young men reported to boot camp, and right after they completed their training, they were sent overseas.

In 1904, my owner Carrie and her husband who kept me in good shape for a decade sold me in early 1914, six months before the war in Europe began on July 28, 1914. Carrie loved being busy and always treated my tenants with respect. If payments were only a week late or ten days later, she patiently waited for the rent. But there was a couple who were forced to move because they fought all the time and tenants were complaining. Others moved out because they could afford to buy or rent a house, and some moved because of a new job or the loss of one. It was sad to see them go, and I hoped my new owner would continue to take good care of me.

It seemed like when Mr. Speziali's Deli moved out of my building, I was filled with anxiety about who my new tenant would be. Speziali's was a fixture in my building since 1902 until 1912. When Mr. Marcuccio's Deli replaced him, his family was kind like the Speziali's and allowed my tenants who were short on money to pay their grocery bills a little at a time. Their deli smelled of Mrs. Marcuccio's simmering spaghetti sauce, including their salami, fresh olives, garlic, hanging provolone cheese, tomatoes, onions, and fresh Italian bread and homemade pastries. It made everyone hungry—including me!

It was now 1917 and World War I was still raging. Patricia and Kathleen were looking for their first full-time jobs and were preparing to move away from me. Two days before the twins moved out, Mrs. Marcuccio came up to their apartment with all the ingredients for her special sauce—which the girls always tried to replicate but couldn't. "I'm gonna show you both," she said in her thick accent. "Someday you gonna teach your bambinos how to make a good sauce. You gonna tell them it's a gift from me." She even shared her secret about adding a pinch of sugar and a piece of hard Romano cheese to the sauce about a half-hour before it was ready to eat. It was hard for the twins to say goodbye. They hugged and kissed Mrs. Marcuccio goodbye and promised to come visit.

I was sad on the day Kathleen and Patricia moved out but grateful because they found two new D'Youville College students, Kate Jorden and Molly Malone, to move into their apartment. It gave me a chance to stay updated about the twins' lives and to learn more about what was happening with the war and the suffragette movement.

I was glad when the twins came to visit the girls and discovered that Patrick and Shawn were sent to the front lines in Europe right after their basic training. The girls were both panicky when they heard the news. They told Kate and Molly about how scared they were. Molly's older brother and Kate's cousin were still fighting on the front lines, and they knew what could happen to their loved ones.

Days of worry turned into weeks and months of stress. On the day World War I ended, November 11, 1918, Kathleen found out that her friend Shawn was wounded and lost his right leg, and he wouldn't be able to come home until he adapted to his artificial limb. Patricia's friend, Patrick, was able to get through the war safely. Becky's brother was coming home with superficial wounds on his upper torso, and Kate's cousin didn't make it home at all. He lost his life the day before the war ended. My heart hurt for all of them and everyone who had to go to war to fight for freedom. Their families and friends would suffer the loss of their loved ones for the rest of their lives. I observed firsthand their pain and anguish. I was frustrated and helpless but grateful I was still connected to the twins and their friends.

. . . .

CHAPTER SIX

The Right to Vote

In 1920, every woman in the country finally won the right to vote, and the twins came back for one more celebration with their friends. At first, it was hard for me to understand that happy and sad things can happen at the same time. The girls cried, laughed, and prayed, knowing this was only the beginning of their next challenge: getting equal rights in the workplace.

Grandpa Duffy, now eighty-eight and in poor health, was the first person they told. He smiled the biggest smile they'd ever seen.

"My darlin' granddaughters, I'm excited for both of you."

"Grandpa, we are proud daughters of Irish immigrants, and you raised us to never give up on our goals. Grandpa, we know Grandma Frances is proud of us because we kept our promise to her."

"I know your Grandma is looking down from heaven and sees two independent strong young women."

Several days later, Grandpa Duffy died peacefully at home surrounded by his entire family. It was the end of an era and the beginning of a new world for American women who finally had the right to vote.

It wasn't long before Kathleen and Patricia came to visit Kate and Molly in their old apartment. They hugged and cried. I listened when the twins talked about Grandpa Duffy and how he influenced their lives. They were happy his wish came true but were heartbroken to lose him and glad he lived long enough to see women receive their right to vote.

It wasn't long before Kathleen accepted a job as a social worker for the newly formed Children's Aid Society for the Prevention of Cruelty to Children. It was a chance for her to work directly with children who had no one to look out for them.

Patricia also came back to say a final goodbye to her college friends. This time Kathleen couldn't come along with her because of her heavy caseload of young children. Patricia told the girls all about her new job as a live-in assistant at Welcome Hall Settlement House, located on the corner of Erie and Canal Streets. The program was founded by Mary Remington, a Massachusetts-born social reformer who worked for the Welcome Hall Movement in New Haven, Connecticut, before establishing the movement in Buffalo.

Patricia's new job was a major adjustment and included social work, administrative responsibilities, including teaching English and other practical skills to immigrant families. Her main goal was to help immigrant families adapt to their new lives in America.

I heard her discuss Mary Remington's dedication to the mainly Sicilian and Italian immigrants in the area. She also told Molly and Kate how Mary had struggled to lease the former railroad terminal, which became Welcome Hall that eventually turned into a horrible, overcrowded tenement house. She finally leased the property in 1898 with $200 and raised the rest in donations.

It took several years before Mary was able to renovate the building with the help of hundreds of volunteers, and now it was clean, spacious, and well-cared for. The tenants loved her for making the building livable for their families.

"In the beginning, I was overwhelmed," Patricia told Molly and Kate, "because there were so many people just struggling to survive. Now, I feel like they're my families, and I understand why they came to be free in America. I love helping them but there is so much work to do . . . and so many hearts to be mended."

Molly and Kate were freshmen working on their teaching degrees at D'Youville College when they met Kathleen and Patricia. It happened when the twins came to visit the campus and to talk about the Suffragette movement. They were volunteer freshmen greeters like Bridget was when they first met her. It didn't take long before Molly and Kate became suffragettes. They wanted to experience living on their own as the twins did. It's how they found out that their apartment was going to be available soon.

Both girls lived in my building for several years, allowing me to keep up-to-date with the twins. I couldn't wait to hear the young women talk about politics and what was happening in their lives.

It was a sad day in September of 1924 when I heard that Mr. Marcuccio passed away, and their deli had to close. Shortly after his death, Mrs. Marcuccio moved out of the city to live with her daughter's family. I missed them both. Lou's Restaurant moved into my building months later. Their food was good, and the sandwiches and soup were affordable, but it was never the same as Mr. Marcuccio's. Molly and Kate graduated from D'Youville College and stayed in their apartment until just after Mr. Marcuccio's closed. It's then that they both got their teaching jobs. My fear now is that I'll never see my Patricia and Kathleen again. During this time, I realized how unpredictable life is and how we constantly lose the people we love. Some might wonder why this story has a lot of death in it, and all I can say is that it's the truth. Death knocks on everyone's door sometime during a lifetime. I'm a building that can listen, observe, and became emotionally attached to my tenants. They taught me over and over what it's like to be human. They are all survivors, and I am too. I'll never have the right to vote, but my twin suffragettes will.

. . . .

CHAPTER SEVEN

Immigrants Unite – Part I

In 1924, a Sicilian father, Anthony Consiglio, and his oldest son, Sammy, moved into my apartment building from the Canal District. I watched as three of their friends from Saint Anthony of Padua Church in downtown Buffalo helped them carry their sparse belongings up to one of two empty second-floor apartments. Their friends spoke broken English, so I couldn't understand everything they were saying, but I do remember their interesting names—Bruno, Carlo, and Gino. They were singing "Amore," a popular Italian song I'd heard other tenants play on the radio, but Anthony and Sammy were merely listening to the song. They both seemed serious and sad.

About a week later, a surprise guest came to visit both men. It was my suffragette, Patricia Duffy. She'd become friends with the Consiglios when they worked on repairing the Welcome Hall Settlement House in the Hooks located in the City of Buffalo's First Ward in the Canal District. It was named after the cargo hook that dockworkers and longshore men used. The area was mostly filled with tenement houses in terrible condition. The living conditions were horrible for poor first generation Sicilian and Italian immigrants. Anthony and Sammy were volunteers at the Settlement House and then, a short time later, were hired as part-time workers. Anthony was a carpenter's helper, and Sammy a plasterer. When Patricia first got hired at Welcome Hall Settlement House, she befriended Mary Remington, a social reformer and founder of the Settlement House, and it's how she was introduced to both of the Consiglios.

When Patricia stopped to visit Kate and Molly, I found out how Anthony and Sammy arrived in Buffalo in 1914 from Palermo, Italy. Maria, Anthony's wife, and their two younger children stayed behind in Italy waiting for them to earn enough money to send for them. They both decided to leave Italy to begin a new life in America because of Sicily's crop failures, high taxes, and unstable government. It must have been horrible to leave the rest of the family behind.

It took them three years until 1917 to send for Anthony's wife Maria and their two younger children. When they arrived in Buffalo, Maria carried with her a small statue of Saint Joseph in her baggage along with a fava bean in her purse for good luck. This tradition was passed on to Maria from her grandparents in Messina, Sicily. Her family were peasant farmers, and the fava bean was fodder for the cattle during a famine. When they had no food to eat, they prepared fava beans to feed their family.

In early 1919, the Consiglio's young daughters, five-year-old Rose and six-year-old Sophia, became sick with influenza. They tried to protect them from the other sick children in the tenement house where they lived, but it was in vain. Both girls had to be hospitalized and died within a week of complications. Maria sobbed and wailed while Anthony and Sammy both shook their heads in disbelief, their hands raised into the air crying out to Saint Joseph, asking "Why? Why?" Then, they held Maria in their arms until their first wave of tears stopped leaving them in total shock.

It wasn't long before Maria got sick and had a terrible time breathing. She too was hospitalized with a poor prognosis. Before she died, she made Anthony promise to save money, buy a home, and marry again—"In honor of me and our babies," she said. "And I want our Sammy to marry and have a family of his own." When I heard about their promise to Maria, I understood why they prayed to Saint Joseph every single day.

It was overwhelming to hear their heartbreaking story. Only there was more sadness to come. I found out that Mrs. Consiglio died with her unborn child only months before the influenza epidemic ended. I kept asking myself, "Why? Why do people have to die?" It's the same question I ask myself over and over. I don't know the answer, but what I do know is that we all grieve in different ways. I know I'm only a building, but somehow I feel their pain and sorrow. Mr. Consiglio was devastated but grateful for the caskets that were given free of charge to his family by the city of Buffalo. They both received support from the Welcome Hall's new Italian Men's Club, which they joined in early 1914 when they first arrived in Buffalo. At the time, the club had fewer than ten members, and everyone paid dues of twenty-five cents a month. They joined because it made them feel safe and supported in their time of need; all the men and their families brought them food to eat, said prayers with them, and provided comfort to them in their time of need.

Anthony's treasured statue of Saint Joseph and Maria's lucky fava bean were kept wrapped in Maria's favorite handkerchief and placed on a small table in the living room. Each night, the father and son promised Saint Joseph they would work hard to save enough money to buy a home. They also vowed to buy a special gravestone for Maria and the children right after they kept their promise to buy a home.

After hearing Patricia tell their story, I thought about the moment I saw them open the door to their apartment. Anthony and Sammy hugged each other and cried. Then, they looked around their small apartment, got on their knees, and prayed. I learned later that it was Gino who convinced Anthony and Sammy to join the Holy Cross Church on the West Side while they were still living in the Hooks. It's there that they prayed to Saint Joseph asking him to help them get a job near their new church. Both men were determined to get full-time jobs and an apartment on the West Side. They were determined to fulfill their promise to Maria. Within a month, Anthony and Sammy joined the Madre Addolorata Society at Holy Cross Church. It was founded by Italian immigrants who banded together to make sure there was a fund available for a proper burial when a member of the society died. The Consiglios were happy to be able to help others like their Welcome Hall's Italian Club members helped them when Marie and the children died.

In 1924, Anthony and Sammy were both hired as laborers digging sewers for the city of Buffalo. It was a dirty, thankless job, but it came with full-time work and a stable paycheck. It's why they could afford to move into my building. Anthony was raised to work hard, and whenever he was tired, he would tell Sammy that their jobs were only a step away from better ones.

Right after the Consiglios moved into my apartment, something terrible happened that affected Anthony's father, who was still in Sicily. It came as a shock when they heard that the Immigration Act of 1924 passed without a struggle in Congress. It caught many Eastern European immigrants by surprise. The Johnson–Reed Act limited the number of immigrants allowed into the United States through a national origins quota. It provided immigration visas to only 2 percent of the total number of people of each nationality in the

United States as of the 1890 national census, excluding immigrants from Asia. Many families were unable to be reunited because of it. It's sad to say that in the winter of that same year, Mr. Consiglio's father Anthony Sr. died in Sicily. His son continued to send a portion of their savings to his Momma, hoping they could someday bring her to America. I'm learning that most of my tenants and their families experienced many tragedies and struggled to move forward with their lives. I'm finding out that sorrow can make a person strong and resilient like me with my solid walls and construction. I can't control anything that might happen to me, but I see firsthand that being a human gives you the ability to survive the unthinkable.

When my new Canadian tenants moved in, I learned that Canadians were exempt from the restrictive Immigration Act and came across the border in great numbers. It's why Louise Williams, a Canadian high school English teacher, moved into my second-floor apartment in early 1924. Louise was in her mid-twenties and had black, curly hair and blue eyes, and she loved teaching at Lafayette High School, only a walking distance away.

When Louise first met her next-door neighbors, Sammy and Anthony, she realized that especially the elder Mr. Consiglio needed to speak better English, and she told them both she would tutor them.

They often asked Miss Louise to read the daily newspaper to them, and sometimes she'd even invite them into her apartment to listen to her new radio. I loved learning about the world outside my walls and wondered what it would be like to experience it firsthand. It made me want to learn more and more. I heard all kinds of music and listened to news and stories that continued week after week. A few months later, Louise's Polish-Canadian friend, Stanislaw Kowalski, a New York Central Railroad detective, moved into her apartment. He was often away for weeks at a time, and when he returned home, he would bring a supply of illegal bootleg liquor to share with my tenants. Everyone waited and was excited to see Stan, and they all carefully hid their illegal gifts.

In 1925, an extremely private Irish family, the Murphys, moved into my other second-floor apartment. They were quiet and kept to themselves. It took a while before I found out their family history, mainly because I was so involved with the Consiglios, Louise Williams, and my other Canadian tenants' lives that I didn't get to spend the time I needed to get to know them personally.

New tenants moved into the empty apartment next to the Irish family in the beginning of 1926. It was two French-Canadian nurses, Sally and Veronica, who worked for the Visiting Nurse Service of New York in The Hooks. The service was one of the oldest not-for-profit home care agencies in the country, operating since 1893. Their founder, Lillian Wald, was the first public health nurse in the United States. Both women constantly worked long hours, both days and nights. I didn't get to know either of them, but I did see them helping to take care of everyone in the building if they had a cold or suddenly became ill.

Earning enough money to save for a home motivated both Anthony and Sammy to work harder. They were proud of their Sicilian heritage and vowed to never give up. When Anthony's job ended, he was hired as a laborer for the Peace Bridge Construction Project, which started in 1925 and was projected to be completed in 1927. Anthony now had two solid years to prove to his employers that he was a hard worker eager to learn new carpentry skills. He was proud to be one of many to watch the first car cross the Peace Bridge on March 13, 1927. It was a beautiful new international bridge between Canada and the United States, situated at the east end of

Lake Erie at the source of the Niagara River. It was named to honor 100 years of peace between the United States and Canada.

The fear of losing their hard-earned money was a constant worry for Anthony and Sammy. In Sicily, the thought of being able to save money in a bank was non-existent. Both father and son put their money inside an old boot in the corner of Anthony's bedroom closet. Weekly, they took the boot out and counted every single penny. I watched how satisfied they were to touch and feel their money, and it gave them hope for the future.

When their boot was filled with bills, they needed to find a new, better hiding place. As their money continued to grow, they exchanged it for larger bills and neatly stacked them in cloth bags. Since Anthony was a new carpenter by trade, he cut out a section of one of their bedroom closet floors to make room for more money and covered it with painted plywood. Every year on Maria's birthday, they'd take the money out of the closet, count it, then carefully place it back into its hiding place.

Mr. Consiglio's prized possession was a battered mandolin given to him by his dear friend Giovanni for repairing his storm-damaged barn. It was a Sicilian twelve-string model. It had three strings per course and had been in the family for years. He told Anthony to take it to America. He said, "Promise me you will learn how to play it and make us Sicilians proud." It was an offer Anthony couldn't refuse. He vowed to someday find someone who could teach him an entire song. Several times a week, I'd hear him try to play his mandolin. I must admit, he needed lessons.

Sammy did most of the cooking, and usually, they ate bread, pasta, lentils, and pasta fagioli. Every couple of weeks, they went out for supper at Santasiero's, an Italian restaurant, a short walking distance away on the corner of Lafayette and Niagara Streets. There they would splurge on their favorite pork chop or steak dinner. The restaurant felt like home because they could talk to other Sicilian people who lived in the neighborhood. When they walked home, they were full and happy.

Once a month, Sammy's father made a huge pot of sauce that would smell delicious, and he would invite his friends in the building to have Sunday dinner with them. Having company reminded them of happier times with Maria and the children. Soon it became a tradition, and everyone brought something to share.

For the next couple of years, Anthony worked a variety of construction jobs. In 1929, he got a lucky break when he was hired as a carpenter to work on Buffalo's new city hall. In the same year, a relative of one of Sammy's Italian Society friends working at the Curtiss-Wright Aeroplane Company, one of the largest manufacturers of aeroplanes in the world gave Sammy an application and a reference for employment, and within a short period of time, he was hired. Both father and son were grateful to have an opportunity of a lifetime to earn a good wage with benefits. Now their savings could grow faster, and they could keep their promise to buy a special gravestone for Maria and the children.

When the stock market crashed in 1929, the bottom fell out of the economy; both men's jobs were still solid, but hundreds of thousands of people were out of work. I listened carefully to the news on the radio and heard how banks already started failing earlier in the decade at a rate of about six hundred per year. Now there was no government denial about being in the middle of a major depression. In fact, the radio and newspapers reported that we were in the middle of a global depression. While European countries were still recovering from the horrible World War 1, America's average workers were losing their homes because of job loss and over-extended credit. Most had no savings left to handle the crisis of unemployment. During this time, I was sad to learn that the Welcome Hall Settlement House, where the Consiglios had first lived, next door to Mary Remington's Mission House, closed their doors.

The Consiglios and Patricia Duffy were heartbroken and upset about the closing of the Mission House for different reasons. For Anthony and Sammy, it was where they learned to adapt to American culture with the support of Mary Remington and her welcoming staff. And for Patricia, it was her first professional job and chance to offer immigrants assistance in all aspects of American life. It made me feel terrible because when my adopted families suffered, I did too.

. . . .

CHAPTER EIGHT

Immigrants Unite – Part II

I was still curious about my private Irish family who lived down the hall from the Consiglios. I decided to try to find out more about who they were and what their lives were like and was glad I had extra time to find out. There was Margaret Murphy, a widowed grandmother, her daughter, Maggie, and her three-year-old granddaughter, Molly. I thought it was strange that all their names began with the letter "M".

It didn't take long to see that Granny Margaret was a strong, opinionated woman who loved to talk about her family's history. I found out that her father, Patrick Haley, died in the Civil War in 1865, right before it ended. He was a member of the famous Irish Brigade, an infantry brigade that served in the Union Army. Their motto was "They shall never retreat from the charge of lances."

When Margaret was growing up, her widowed mother, Mary, was left alone to care for her when she was only two years old. Struggling to survive, Mary took in boarders to make ends meet. But her luck changed when her Aunt Becca moved in to take care of her little daughter, Margaret, while she worked as a chambermaid to supplement her small widow's Civil War pension.

I discovered Margaret's generation was the first to traditionally name a "first" daughter with a name starting with the letter "M". This was significant because it stood for the word miracle. It was a priceless gift of hope. When Margaret grew up and had her own daughter, she named her Maggie. When Maggie was old enough, she told her to let the letter "M" in her name inspire her to have hope and believe in miracles.

I often heard Margaret tell Maggie that they were survivors who at last had a nice apartment in a real neighborhood. "Finally," she'd say, "we can take my granddaughter, Molly, for a walk safely without being afraid."

Maggie worked as a charwoman in a public elementary school and as a maid on the weekends. She was constantly tired and knew she had to get a better job where she could make more money and have time to spend with her daughter, Molly. One day, Maggie stayed home from work in order to fill out job applications at nearby restaurants. She hoped and prayed she'd get hired at Deco's Restaurant for the night shift.

Soon I found out the secrets they never told anyone. They wouldn't have liked it if they knew I was listening. It's when I discovered Maggie never had a husband. It was a lie they both needed to keep. Both mother and daughter made it a habit of burying that fact. It was only on rare occasions when Margaret and Maggie were alone that they talked together openly about their past. Once I heard the truth, I felt bad for them and understood why they didn't tell the real story. They were so petrified about what people would think about their family if they knew what really happened. It's why they made up a tale way before Molly was born to save them from all the judgments.

The truth was that Maggie's boyfriend left her immediately when he learned she was having his baby. He was also a drinker and never held a steady job, mainly because he would often go to work drunk. He could only get hired and fired. Maggie couldn't afford to keep their small apartment on her own and as soon as Molly was born, she moved out and into her mother's rooming house. Then, they had to move out because the owner charged more rent. They never told anyone about what happened, and Maggie never referred to her fake husband by name. She simply called him not by name, but by "he." They told the story so many times they almost believed it themselves.

The truth was too painful.

In real life, Maggie got pregnant, and her boyfriend left her when he found out. Most girls in those days were sent away immediately by their families to put their baby up for adoption or to have an abortion. Having an unmarried, pregnant daughter was considered a horrible disgrace. Maggie's mother refused to let that disgrace happen to her only daughter. But what they did do was to move from apartment to apartment right before they were evicted for not paying their rent on time. Right before they moved into my building, they had lived in one of the shabbiest and most crowded tenement buildings in the Canal District. They saved every penny they could for an entire year so they could afford a modest apartment.

Grandma Margaret believed in the power of prayer, and even in the middle of the worst of times, she remembered how her own mother Mary prayed every day to her prized statue of the Virgin Mary Mother of God. Great-Grandma Mary's own mother carried it with her and her husband when they escaped from County Cork, Ireland, in the late 1850s. This same statue gave Grandma Margaret and her daughter the courage they needed to survive their troubled times. Being able to afford to live in one of my apartments was the miracle they'd prayed for.

The Virgin Mary must have listened to their prayers again because Maggie was hired as a waitress immediately after she applied at Deco's. It was Deco's first restaurant on West Eagle Street, on the corner of Pearl. She worked the busy late-night shift, and her tips were generous. She waited on all types of people, rich and poor, young and old, healthy and sick. The restaurant was a favorite of cops and the homeless because they could get a good cup of coffee for five cents and a hamburger for a dime. Men and teenage boys at Deco's flirted with Maggie, but she never dated anyone. Maggie didn't have the time or the interest. She told herself it really didn't matter, but what did matter was saving money and caring for little Molly and Momma.

Deco Restaurant – Seneca and Burch Streets.
Collection of The Buffalo History Museum.
Goldome/Nagle photograph collection, Picture. G65, Streets.

Saving money was important to both women. Deco's was the perfect fit for Maggie, and now she no longer had to clean other people's houses. She kept praying that someday her mother could also leave her domestic job and make more money too.

Margaret's Grandma Mary's family emigrated from County Cork, Ireland, to America in the late 1850s to keep their family from starving from hunger or illness during the Potato Famine. When they were home in Ireland, they were a farming family, working for an English landowner.

Margaret often told Maggie the story of her parents and how they were hardy and strong souls. When they first came to America, they left all their belongings behind. They traveled with only their suitcases across the Irish Sea to Liverpool in northwest England, then to America into New York City, then onto Buffalo, New York, and ended up in the low-lying area south of the city near the waterfront called "Shanty Town."

"In the 1850s, when they first arrived in Buffalo," Margaret would explain, "there were no steady jobs. Unemployment was high, and no one welcomed the Irish. Your Great-Grandpa Haley had to take all the hard labor jobs he could. Most were seasonal. He helped build roads, canals, and bridges. When the Civil War started, your great-grandpa wanted to prove he was a good American, and that's why he joined the Union Army. Only he died too soon. Your great-grandma Mary made sure I didn't go hungry and prayed to live long enough to see her future grandchildren, and Mary, the Blessed Virgin made sure I did."

Like the Consiglios, the Murphys didn't believe in banks. Grandma Margaret ripped open the seam in the bottom of their worn-out couch to hide their money. Both women took all their change, turned it into bills, and stuffed it inside their new "money" couch.

They did this after breakfast, each Sunday morning. I watched as they carefully counted their change and inserted the new "money" into the couch with coffee cups in hand. They would look at each other and smile knowing their future was brighter. Often, they let little Molly help, too. She got to gather up all the pennies in one big pile.

On Sundays, they'd take long walks with Molly—it was a time to be grateful. They would explore their new neighborhood and talk with neighbors who were sitting outside. It also gave Grandma Margaret time to rest before she made her special Sunday dinner. Each week, Margaret and Maggie would wait for little Molly's plea right after breakfast. "Momma walk. Momma walk," she'd say, tugging on Maggie's cotton dress. I would wait to hear one of them tell Molly to go get her coat. Then, off they'd go enjoying each other's company, although Grandma Margaret always came home first to begin cooking a small roast beef or chicken, mashed potatoes, and peas. If she had time, she would also make a loaf of homemade bread or maybe oatmeal cookies for dessert.

It was now 1930, and Anthony and Sammy had never met their other second-floor tenants because they were both up and out before dawn and home after dusk, except in the winter when it was dark. Then, they had their weekly English class with Louise, church, Sunday dinner, and occasional Italian Society meetings. Early one Sunday morning, Sammy was opening their stuck kitchen window when he noticed a pretty young woman walking by with a small child. She stopped right in front of the building and was talking to Louise, his English teacher.

He couldn't take his eyes off her. *I wonder if she lives in my building*, he thought. The following Sunday, he rushed home from church and told his father he felt like going for a short walk. Every Sunday, he started going for a walk right after they came home from Holy Cross Church. When Sammy saw Maggie and her little girl, he would smile and say hello. Gradually, they made small talk, and he found out they both lived in the same building and on the same floor.

When Sammy first saw Maggie and Molly walking in front of me, I could tell that he was attracted to her. There was something about her that made her special. I remember this because when he first told his father about Maggie, I heard Anthony ask Sammy, "Is she Italian?" When Sammy said, "No, she's Irish," Anthony yelled at him, "You have to fall in love with an Italian woman, not an Irish one."

It's funny now because at the time Maggie's mother felt the same way about Italian men. I smiled to myself knowing I was responsible for the beginning of a love affair between two young people who experienced great personal sadness in their short lifetimes.

Sammy never had time for a girlfriend, and Maggie vowed to give up men forever. It took Sammy a couple of months to even mention Maggie to his father. He already knew he'd be angry because she wasn't a nice Sicilian girl. Maggie didn't tell her mother about Sammy for a couple of months either, knowing she would not be happy to find out she was interested in a Sicilian man. Meanwhile, Sammy had to deal with his father's anger, and Maggie had to deal with her mother's ranting too.

"Papa, she's only a friend; she's nice and a good mother to her daughter Molly. She's divorced and works hard to support her.

They're like us, Papa. Trying to get ahead, saving money, and trying to better themselves. They're just like us, Papa."

"No, Sammy. I don't like it. We don't mix!"

"Papa, we are in America. We are alike. We're immigrants. Please, Papa, let's invite them here for Sunday dinner. Saint Joseph will be upset with you for your closed mind."

"Sammy, I'll pray about it, but I don't know if I can do it."

"Our family died, Papa, and we have each other, but we need to make more friends. We came to America to be free. Momma would understand, and Saint Joseph would too."

Sammy's father eventually relented and agreed to make a big spaghetti dinner.

It didn't take long before Sammy and Maggie were spending more time together. Little by little, I could see their attraction toward each other grow. Soon, Sammy, Maggie, and Molly were taking walks together. When I saw them walking toward me, they were smiling, laughing, and holding hands. Then, I saw them kissing in my hallway. I couldn't believe it! I was watching a young couple fall in love—something I would never be able to do. I wondered what a kiss would feel like. It seemed like it was something magical. When I came back to reality, I was happy for the three of them because maybe someday Sammy would become Molly's father.

Both families continued to enjoy their Sunday dinners together. Grandma Margaret even hosted an occasional Irish Sunday dinner for everyone, too.

The Consiglios' money grew into thousands of dollars, and they knew they would soon be able to buy a two-flat house with a cottage in the rear for extra income. Life was getting better for both men. Anthony met a young Italian widow with three small children at church and began an official courtship with her. Her husband was an Italian immigrant who was killed in a trolley accident in 1924. Their relationship brought back memories of Maria and his babies, and he knew it was time to fulfill his promise to Maria.

Being with Jane, his widow's American name, and her children, made Anthony feel loved again, and it would give him a chance to help raise another family who needed him. He told Sammy that Jane agreed to marry him as soon as he could buy them their own home. The timing was perfect because Sammy told his Papa he had asked Maggie to marry him as soon as they could purchase a double family home with a cottage in the back.

"If you agree, Papa, Maggie's mother, Margaret, could move into the small cottage behind our big house. She can pay us a reasonable rent."

"Yes, my son, we will all become part of a new American family."

I was happy for the Consiglios and Murphys and sad that I'd probably never see them again. My only consolation was that I knew both families had heartaches in their lives and now it was time for new beginnings.

America was still in trouble, and I couldn't help but listen to the news on Louise's radio when everyone came home from work. She even let tenants go into her apartment to listen when she was working. It was the worst of times for our country, and all I could do was watch events unfold through the lives of my tenants. I wished I had the power to make the world a better place for everyone.

Somehow all my tenants kept their jobs through this hard time. Louise still taught, and Stan was busier than ever, checking railroad boxcars for desperately homeless vagrants going from place to place in search of jobs, food, and shelter. Little Molly was now eleven years old and happy to have Sammy in her life, and when Grandma

Margaret smothered her with kisses, she'd ask, "Grandma, why do you give me sloppy kisses?"

"Because I love you, Molly. It's my way of showing you how I feel."

When I heard the two of them talking about sloppy kisses, I saw how much they loved each other, and I wanted one too.

Soon Anthony and Sammy were able to apply for their U.S. citizenship and completed their petitions for naturalization in 1931. This included extensive interviewing and English and civics tests. Both men prayed for the opportunity to take an oath of allegiance. When they received their approval in the mail, they dropped down on their knees and thanked St. Joseph.

Everyone was proud of them, and all the tenants came together in their apartment to celebrate their American citizenship and naturalization. They sat around the crowded table, ate Italian food, drank some wine, and shared in the joy of citizenship. Louise Williams, their special friend and teacher, arranged for them to speak to her English class. They couldn't wait to show the class their Permanent Resident card. Anthony and Sammy worked hard to learn English and become Americans. I admired them for never giving up. I also shared their sorrow over the loss of their family and felt sad to hear them cry in the privacy of their apartment. Little did they know how much they taught me about the power of love and how eternal it is in the face of death.

Now it was time for Anthony to keep his promise to his friend Giovanni back in Sicily. He had finally saved enough money to purchase a third edition of Salvator Léonardi's book entitled *Method for Banjolin and Mandolin-Banjo in English, French, and Spanish.* Anthony vowed to learn how to play Mario's mandolin and make Sicilians proud. He couldn't wait to see if he could play it for the

Holy Cross Church members for their special occasions and honor his friend back home in Sicily.

Even my Irish family was fortunate during the Great Depression because Deco's continued to make money, and Maggie's job stayed solid. The restaurant was important to all kinds of people—coffee was still five cents and hamburgers a dime. In 1930, Deco's Restaurant moved closer to home on Niagara and Georgia Street, and Maggie was able to walk to work. The restaurant was constantly crowded, and she made good tips, and it was a wonderful employer.

Grandma Margaret lost her job as a domestic but was able to get a job at Deco's working an early-afternoon shift. My visiting nurses kept their jobs, too. Everyone was happy and grateful to be working. Meanwhile, Anthony and Sammy bought the double house with a carriage house in the back, in 1933. For them, it was a dream come true. It was located on Seventh Street, and they purchased it for $2,800.00. Anthony married Jane, and Sammy married Maggie, but before she married him, she told him the truth about never being married. She explained to him that they had to do it to protect their family from gossip. They didn't trust anyone and had to keep neighbors from asking questions about why little Molly had no father. At first, Sammy was shocked, but he understood the reason and was glad he was going to be her first real husband and father of her child.

"Molly's mine," he said proudly. "I'm going to adopt her."

Grandma Margaret was excited too because now she had her own small carriage house right behind that of her new family.

I was happy to see how all their lives meshed together as a blended family. It made me proud. I knew how fortunate the Consiglios felt to be able to keep their promise to Maria, and the Murphys would no longer have to live a lie. Maggie found the love of her life and a father Molly could be proud of. I couldn't ask for more for my special tenants who'd created a wonderful life after many hardships and losses. It was great to see my immigrants appreciate their diversity.

CHAPTER NINE

. . . .

Survivors of the Pale of Russia

By the end of 1933, I noticed something strange. The owner of my building was no longer coming to visit me. No one came to clean the halls or the stairs. I was empty, with no business on the first floor. I was abandoned. Then, the notices arrived, and Louise, her friend Stan Stanislaw, and the two nurses were evicted. They were all upset; they couldn't believe it. They had to move as soon as possible because of my emergency foreclosure.

I was alone and empty for the first time in my life. My family of tenants was no longer in my building. It was silent, except for me. I felt lost and standing empty on the corner of Niagara Street and Potomac Avenue. I began thinking about Grandpa Duffy, the Consiglio family tragedy, and how over time I lost track of my Abigail and her family. I relived the histories of all my tenants and understood how it must have felt when they were all faced with losses they had no control over.

My prayers were answered in 1935 when Mr. Steel bought my building at an auction. Immediately, he started cleaning and repairing me. Mr. Steel was a contractor/carpenter, and it was good to feel important again. I was being rented and was grateful to begin another new chapter in my life. I couldn't wait to see what the future held for me.

Two tenants moved in right after Mr. Steel finished with my rehabilitation in 1935. It was David Abramovich, a forty-year-old Russian Jew, and his forty-one-year-old cousin Samuel Jaroslow. They moved into my fourth-floor apartment. I'll never forget how excited I was.

The cousins had arrived in Buffalo on a New York Central boxcar at the Lackawanna Station in 1934. They came in desperation to search for Samuel's father's cousin, Jacob Levanski, who left Russia with his young wife twenty-nine years earlier. A crumpled, faded letter postmarked from Buffalo, New York, in 1905 was the only hope they had left. Maybe if they could find Jacob, he'd help them find work.

David and Samuel rode railroad boxcars nationwide for three years, sleeping under bridges, standing in soup lines, and trying to mend their socks and clothes. Sometimes they worked as day laborers on farms, in warehouses, or in stockyards, and they were only two of hundreds of thousands of desperate and unemployed immigrant workers searching for employment.

During those years, they dug through hundreds and hundreds of trash cans, hoping to find discarded newspapers, looking for information about what was happening in America and Eastern Europe.

David and Samuel both cried until they couldn't when they left their fathers behind in their overcrowded and deplorable settlement house east of the New York City's Bowery district. They promised Josef and Abraham, their fathers, that they would return as soon as possible and take them to a real home of their own. Their fathers couldn't go with them because they were too old to travel in boxcars from state to state. Both men gave their sons their blessings and told them not to worry because they were still working together in the same clothing factory and would take care of each other. Before they left, Abraham gave his son his treasured letter from Jacob, and they all prayed they would all be reunited someday.

When both men first moved into their apartment, it was hard for me to understand what they were saying. But it wasn't long before David and Samuel began speaking to each other in English rather than in Yiddish. It took me a while before I grasped what they were saying, but I was glad they were fast learners and determined to become American citizens. Gradually, I learned the reason why hundreds of thousands of Jews fled from Russia to America. Most of those immigrants landed in New York City's lower East Side in the 1800s. The Abramovich and Jaroslow blended families escaped from Russia after years of planning. The Russian Government and officials tried to make the Jews give up their culture and their shtetls—small-town Jewish communities that grew up in Eastern Europe prior to the Holocaust. Thousands of shtetls were located near rivers and lakes in the territory bounded by the Black and Baltic Seas, and the Vistula and Dnieper River basins, with economies based on trade with countryside peasants.

In their shtetl, no one ever felt alone or without community support, and families lived in the same shtetl for generations, often with three generations living under the same roof.

Both the Abramovich and Jaroslow families left their community near the Black Sea early in the 1890s and settled in the city of Moscow, shortly before the second wave of riots in Russia in 1903. David's father, Josef Abramovich, a Russian Jew, was born in Vilma, Russia, in 1868. Josef's brother-in-law Abraham Jaroslow, a Polish Jew, was married to Josef's sister Alina. Both men were good friends, the same age, and successfully employed. Josef became a wealthy cloak-maker with his own business and a home that he owned. Abraham had a tailor shop and home, too.

Still, both men were considered foreigners in their own country, mainly because they spoke only Yiddish and didn't embrace the Russian culture. Both families were forced to leave their businesses and homes and had to move to Central Russia, with nothing but their lives.

Everything changed after Czar Nicholas began his anti-Jewish campaign, called the Pale of Russia, which determined that the Jews had to learn to keep to themselves with no help from the Russian Government. All European Jews were totally segregated into inner-city ghettoes or small shtetl villages with no way to earn a living. They were not allowed to be farmers and had to endure surprise attacks by their non-Jewish neighbors. Riots broke out in many Russian cities, and Jews were stoned, beaten, and their houses burned to the ground.

In 1909, Josef's wife Yetta died, yet he still decided to follow through on their plan to escape Russia with his son David and daughter Rachel. He also left behind his elderly mother and father. They fled by night with Abraham and his son, Samuel. Abraham had to leave Alina, his wife, and their two little girls behind promising to send for them as soon as possible.

On the night the families left, they were fortunate to escape the Russian guards and gangs of murderers, bribing officials along the way. Their passage to Western Europe was an answer to their prayers, and the weeklong voyage to America was a miracle. They never wanted to go back to where they were born and saw America as their new homeland.

The family of five arrived in America without money and spoke no English. The only prized possession they had was the letter from Abraham's cousin Jacob.

This new extended family had freedom in their bones. Josef and Abraham had no idea what the American culture was like or what it would be like working in an industrial environment. Still, coming to this county gave them all hope for a better life. When they got off the ship in New York, the family kissed the ground and cried. When they arrived at the East End of New York's Bowery District, they were directed to the middle of the garment district in the old German section of New York. There were rows of tenement buildings three and four stories high. Each member of the family was willing to take any work that was offered to them. In fact, I found out that the hundreds of thousands of Jews who fled from Russia were living here in deplorable conditions. In Russia, they ate black bread and had clean air to breathe; in the Bowery District, they still had the bread, but the air was dangerous from all the factory emissions. Still, the bottom line was that they were in a free country and could work extra hard to rise above the poverty level.

With the help of the Landsmannschaften, a mutual benefit society organized by Jewish immigrants to help poor newcomers obtain housing and jobs, the family found affordable housing in a small flat among the rows of tenement buildings. It had narrow halls and moldy walls, and the building was unheated in the winter and hot in the summer. The smells were terrible, and the drainage was even worse.

Rooming House Interior, ca. 1900.
Collection of The Buffalo History Museum. Children's Aid Society
photograph collection, Picture. C45, Buildings–Interior.

One by one, they began working in a tenement sweatshop—and there were many to choose from. Papa Josef was the first to be hired in the needle trades. His job was in one of the rooms of a tenement owner's apartment. It had no windows or ventilation, and he worked six days a week, twelve to sixteen hours a day. Abraham was next, followed by David and Samuel. Young Rachel worked, too, and was paid $4 or $5 per week while the men earned six to ten dollars weekly. If anyone complained, though, they were fired and replaced immediately.

Over time, they discovered that their new Jewish community had a Yiddish daily newspaper called the *Foreword*, and it published news from Europe and New York City. It also had advice for new immigrants. David, Samuel, and their fathers would read these papers over and over.

The Yiddish theater continued to survive in the Bowery, and when possible, it allowed the family to escape from their hard work and constant struggles. There, they could see Yiddish adaptations of Shakespeare, Chekov, slapstick comedies, and folk tales. During this time, Jewish writers were creating short stories and fictional novels in English, and non-Jews were beginning to learn and appreciate the Jewish culture.

As soon as David's sister Rachel, and one of Samuel's friends, Peril, turned sixteen, they were hired to work on the ninth floor of the Triangle Shirtwaist Company in the Asch Building in the Greenwich Village area of New York City. They worked nine hours a day on weekdays and seven hours on Saturday, earning between $7 and $12 a week. If they were five minutes late, their pay was docked, and they even had to pay for the needles they used for sewing shirts.

Then, it happened. It was 4:30 p.m. on Saturday, March 25, 1911, when a fire flared up at the Triangle Factory. It started in the scrap bin under one of the cutter's tables on the eighth floor. It was unthinkable, a tragedy beyond belief. Several hundred workers were trapped in the burning building. One hundred forty-six people died without a chance to escape because the exit doors were locked to allow women's purses to be checked as they left the building after work. Even though there were several exits, flames prevented most from escaping through the stairway.

When Josef, Abraham, David, and Samuel heard about the fire, they rushed to the scene, panic-stricken. It was gut-wrenching to know that Rachel and Peril were inside the burning building. When they arrived, some of those trapped were jumping out of the windows. It was a nightmare they would never forget. Hours later, they learned that Rachel and Samuel's friend, Peril, were both dead. Their blended families were shattered.

During the next four years, they struggled to save enough money to move out of the New York City Jewish Settlement. Josef and Abraham continued working in a cloak factory and still held onto their Yiddish language, while David and Samuel were determined to be fluent in English and become American citizens.

Both cousins became activists in the Amalgamated Clothing Workers of America. They wanted to do all they could to make life better for all factory workers. They did not want the deaths of Rachel and Peril to be in vain. As the economy weakened in the late 1920s and the stock market crashed in 1929, the union activists were the first to lose their jobs.

David and Samuel left New York City in search of employment in 1931. They carried with them their special lined sacks containing a few of their prized religious possessions. They knew they would no longer be able to maintain the strict religious practices of Orthodox Jews, who must live in an existing Jewish community. While traveling in boxcars, both men had their own Yiddish Siddur prayer books, which they used to say their prayers early in the morning, before noon when possible, and early in the evening.

Once they arrived in Buffalo, it took two weeks of searching before they found cousin Jacob living in the Canal District on Dante Street. He greeted both men with tears, bear hugs, and blessings in Yiddish. Jacob took them home to his crowded, tiny tenement apartment, and his wife and adult daughters cried and welcomed them into their home.

"You're family," Jacob said. "We make room for you until you get jobs."

The cousins slept on cots pushed up against a living room wall and were grateful. Cousin Jacob was a well-known peddler, who sold his Yankee Notions up and down Niagara Street on the West Side of Buffalo.

He let David and Samuel help him sell his wares while they were looking for jobs. He also learned about potential full-time jobs under President Franklin D. Roosevelt's New Deal Works Projects Administration (WPA) and promised to get them applications. Meanwhile, he accepted no money from them, allowing them to save for an apartment. It was the beginning of a series of lucky breaks for the cousins.

Jacob had a heap of an old black car. It was scratched and dented, and his customers could hear him coming down the street because it had no muffler. They loved him and called him "Itchy." He sold household needs, including aprons, pillowcases, house dresses, dishes, towels, bedspreads, and curtains. Jacob would run up the staircase to each apartment, carrying a large blanket stuffed with merchandise. When an apartment door opened or was already open, he would spread all his merchandise out on the floor in front of the tenants.

If Jacob's customers couldn't pay on the spot, he would let them take the item they wanted and put their name on a piece of paper promising to pay in installments each week. He trusted everyone.

David and Samuel would crouch down in the front and back seat of the car while piles of Jacob's goods were laid on top of them. It was the only way the three of them could fit into the car. Both cousins helped him reach many customers at the same time because they each used a separate blanket filled with merchandise.

"Itchy's here!" someone in the hall would yell and up went Jacob first. His tall, thin body, thick black hair, and big smile made everyone he met feel good. He received the respect he never had in his own country and was thankful for their business.

Soon, both David and Samuel were hired as laborers under Roosevelt's WPA program. They were going to be helping to build Buffalo's Civic Stadium, which was scheduled to be completed in 1938. They would earn $41.57 per month . It was still considered a low wage, but to them, it felt like a million bucks because their vagrant days of riding boxcars were over. It was their first solid full-time job since they had left home three years ago.

Almost every extra penny the cousins earned was saved for a deposit on an apartment of their own but only after they sent money home to their fathers. Jacob found out about my empty apartment, which offered reasonable rent, from one of his favorite customers.

David and Samuel couldn't wait to rent the apartment because it was a neighborhood they felt comfortable in and knew most of the residents. When the cousins moved in, they had nothing but the clothes on their backs, two thin blankets, tin plates, cups, forks, a metal pot and knife, and their treasured sack filled with religious items. Jacob helped the cousins get third-hand furniture and charged them a fair price. Their apartment cost $15 per month with a seven-dollar deposit. It was furnished with an icebox, cooled with a twenty-five-cent block of ice every other day. It also had a coal stove and their first pull chain toilet, which they had to learn to use.

Now, because of their new full-time jobs, they could no longer celebrate the Sabbath, the Jewish day of worship, which is observed from sundown on Friday until Saturday. During this time, they would normally not be permitted to work, cook, drive, use electricity, or touch money.

What the cousins did do was to prepare for Friday's Sabbath on Wednesdays and Thursdays. After saying their evening prayers and using their tattered prayer shawls, they would share one Tehillim Psalm book and take turns reading a few chapters. Most importantly, though, they had their cherished Torah containing rules for daily life, how to worship, what to eat, wear, and how to do business.

They made food for Friday and ate it cold in their dark apartment. When they left for work on Friday mornings, they took their money out of their pockets. They left a couple of hours early, walked to their jobs at Civic Stadium, and walked home at night exhausted. David and Samuel tried their best to honor the Sabbath and were happy to give up using money and comfort on the Sabbath.

On Jewish holidays, Jacob invited David and Samuel to dinner, and when they needed a good meal, they ate supper at Santasiero's on Niagara Street. The food wasn't kosher, but it was good and cheap, and it filled their bellies after a long workday. Eating kosher daily was difficult for them because of its requirements. Their fish couldn't have fins or scales. Meat and milk needed to be from animals that didn't chew cud or have split hoofs and were slaughtered according to Jewish law. Birds of prey could not be eaten. They did what they could do to honor their faith and hoped to someday be able to honor the Sabbath properly. Eventually, they did find a kosher deli on the West Side and bought meats and black bread when they could afford it.

One afternoon, David and Samuel came home with a radio, and I was shocked. Jacob found a used one at a cheap price and gave it to them. They both believed having a radio would help them to learn more English. It also gave them a chance to hear the news reports about what was happening in Eastern Europe. I learned a lot, too.

One day, David received an unexpected letter. It was from David's father telling him his grandmother died in her sleep and his grandpa was near death too. The envelope also contained a folded up letter from his grandpa with a message. "Please tell David and Samuel I love them and will be with them in spirit. God Bless America."

The cousins continued to save money to bring Samuel's sisters to America before it was too late to get them out of Russia. The same Johnson Immigration Law that impacted the Consiglios also drastically limited the number of Eastern European immigrants and made it almost impossible to bring them into the country. It was twenty-five years since they'd last seen Samuel's mother and sisters and David's elderly grandparents. Letters did arrive every few months from the sisters, but they were barely surviving in the same shtetl.

Jacob's "Yankee Notions" peddler business generated a good income, and he saved every penny he could as well. He was able to finally look for a house on the West Side where he had most of his customers and hoped to open a small furniture store. Jacob would tell both cousins that their papas could even work part-time in his store if they wanted to.

David and Samuel were now coming to the end of their Civic Stadium jobs and were applying for new WPA jobs. Their current employers gave them both excellent references because they appreciated their hard work, flexibility regarding working overtime, and willingness to do any job required of them.

During these three years, the cousins saved $2,500 in a joint savings account at the Manufacturers and Traders Trust Company. At first, it was hard for them to put their money in a bank because of the thousands of banks that had failed during the twenties. Their supervisor, Mr. Beam, encouraged them to use a bank and warned them about keeping cash in their apartment. He told them it was too risky, in case of a theft or a fire. At first, they checked with the bank weekly to make sure their money was still safe. Then gradually, the cousins only checked their deposits once a month.

Their foreman told both men he would vouch for them and get them applications for new jobs working on the Buffalo Zoological Gardens.

Founded in 1875, the zoo quickly expanded, and both the Zoological Society and the city of Buffalo planned a major renovation with help from the WPA program. David and Samuel would be helping to construct new buildings on the property at Parkside and Colvin.

From David and Samuel, I understood how despair for the Eastern European Jews hit them hard during their time riding boxcars throughout the country. They cried and continued praying for the safety of all the Jews fleeing for their lives and for those who were now being captured and killed by the rise of Nazi power. Over and over, I learned how each new immigrant population had to overcome prejudice and adversity before they integrated into the American Society.

David and Samuel made no new friends in my building because they had no time and didn't trust anyone—except for their work supervisor, Mr. Beam, who became a mentor and helped them learn many new construction skills. Mr. Beam's advice and contacts in the WPA was an answer to their prayers.

While the cousins were learning English at home, they were also enrolled in a Wednesday evening class at Lafayette High School where they learned English and American history in preparation for citizenship. During this time, a letter arrived for Samuel from his father, and his heart sank. I saw the look of fear on his face, and he instantly turned pale. He held the envelope in his shaking hands before he opened it. In it, Samuel read that his mother had died a month earlier of influenza. Their happiness quickly evaporated into grief. Both men's mothers were gone, along with David's sister, Rachel, and Samuel's friend, Peril. They vowed that they would send for Samuel's sisters before it was too late.

. . . .

CHAPTER TEN

The Long Road to Citizenship

Something unusual happened on the first night of David and Samuel's citizenship class at Lafayette High School. The cousins recognized and were introduced to three other tenants who lived in the same apartment down the hall from them on the third floor. Dominic Schiavone, his son Antonio, and grandson, Angelo, were among the small group of student immigrants who were told to introduce themselves to each other.

Dominic, the seventy-four-year-old grandfather, was taking the class and his son Antonio and grandson Angelo were there to be supportive. When Dominic introduced himself to the class, he told everyone he wanted to become an American citizen before he died.

That evening, they all walked home together after class, and right before David and Samuel reached their apartment, Antonio said, "Come have Sunday dinner with us. My wife, Teresa, will be happy to meet new friends."

Angelo added with a smile, "Papa makes good sauce and Momma makes the best pasta." Then, he put his fingers up to his lips and kissed the air.

"You both come to dinner. You gonna love my red wine. We have good food for you. We gonna be American citizens and friends," Dominic said in broken English.

David and Samuel were anxious when they were invited for dinner but knew it would be rude to refuse. Never in their lives had outsiders wanted to be friends with their Jewish neighbors. It was unusual in Russia; their neighbors and countrymen betrayed them.

"David, if we are going to be American citizens, we have to make new friends, and they don't care if we're Jewish. We have to go." When I heard the cousins talk, I realized it was the first time in their lives that they felt accepted and knew in their hearts that America was destined to be their home country.

On the following Sunday afternoon, both cousins cleaned up, collected their chairs, and walked down the short hall to their first dinner invitation. But before they left their apartment, they prayed for forgiveness for not eating kosher and breaking Jewish law. They knew it was something they had to do if they were going to be Americanized. When they were able to afford their own house, they could again eat kosher, go to temple, and honor the Sabbath. Both men realized that their religious beliefs would have to be modified for the next few years. And this Sunday dinner was a milestone in their lives.

After a quick knock on the door, it opened to four smiling faces and complimentary kisses. Mrs. Teresa Schiavone was the best sight of all and a reminder of their own mothers and treasured sisters. David's mother's death and the loss of his sister, Rachel, in the Triangle Factory Fire left an irreplaceable hole in his heart. Samuel's mother had died too, but his two sisters were still waiting for their freedom in Russia. To see this welcoming mother made them desperately miss their own families.

The Schiavone's preparation for this Sunday's dinner was extra special because they were serving Grandpa Dominic's homemade Sicilian sausage. When they all sat down to dinner, they toasted their new friendship and blessed the food. Teresa's fresh-baked bread was warm, crusty, and spongy on the inside. Dominic's red wine warmed the cousins' insides. The dinner ended with a mouthwatering granita, a semi-frozen dessert made from sugar, water, and various flavorings, originally from Sicily and reserved only for honored guests.

Time passed quickly. Both David and Samuel offered to help clean up but were politely refused. After dinner, the Schiavone family began talking about why they came to America and what it was like living in Buffalo's Canal District. I listened and tried to put myself in their shoes, but of course, it was impossible.

Twenty-eight-year-old Antonio and twenty-five-year-old Teresa Schiavone arrived in Buffalo from Serradifalco, Sicily, province of Caltanissetta, from peasant families who were barely surviving. Antonio's father Dominic was left behind in Sicily waiting until they could afford to send for him. He had been a widower since Antonio was a baby. Dominic's mother raised Antonio until she also died when he was twelve, and Teresa was raised by her maternal grandmother who vowed to never leave Sicily.

Brothers Vito and Enrico Schiavone, Antonio's uncles, arrived in Buffalo, New York, in 1909. The uncles did heavy outside work as dock laborers on the Erie Canal. It wasn't steady employment, and, in the summers, they worked outside of Buffalo on farms and in canneries. It took the brothers four years to save enough money to send for their nephew Antonio and his wife Teresa. They sent the young couple about a hundred lire each for their passage to America.

When Antonio and Teresa arrived in Buffalo, it wasn't long before Antonio was hired for seasonal work, sweeping streets, and raking leaves. They also shared three tenement rooms on the Revere Block in the Canal District with Uncle Enrico, his wife, and three kids.

Teresa was immediately hired as a maid at the Hotel Worth, in 1915. It was the same year their first son Angelo was born, and his baby brother Mario arrived three years later. Both parents were determined to learn English and become American citizens as soon as possible. Their young boys were taught only English because the Schiavones wanted them to be Americanized. They found an English tutor parishioner from Mt. Carmel Church who volunteered to help them prepare for citizenship classes, and little Angelo spoke only English growing up. He learned no Sicilian.

After living in their uncle's tenement building for several years, the Schiavones saved enough money to send for Grandpa Dominic in 1920. He arrived penniless but was still healthy enough to work as a laborer on the New York Central tracks. The hard labor he did back in Sicily kept him strong enough to work a few more years in America.

Once the family saved enough money, they moved to another tenement on Fly Street with only the four of them—rather than ten—living together. Still, the building they moved into was dirty, had bad drainage, filthy halls, and unhealthy air. Again, they saved money and deposited it into the nearest bank, hoping they would someday be able to move out of the Canal District for good. If they could move to the West Side of Buffalo in a residential and industrial neighborhood, they believed they could find full-time jobs and save to buy a real home of their own.

"Momma, remember when I was ten and me and my friends ran after the coal trucks on Erie Street trying to catch pieces of coal dropping on the street?" Angelo said, laughing as he told his story. "We'd even jump up on the truck and open the coal chutes if we could. Then, when we had enough for a bushel, we'd sell it for twenty cents."

"I remember. Your hands and face were always black with coal dust!" Mrs. Schiavone said, smiling.

"Papa, when I was little and asked you for five cents for candy, you'd hold out your closed fist. I'd open it, and it was empty, and you'd say, 'Angelo, you get nothing because there's nothing to give.' Then, when I was old enough, I sold papers and shined shoes to make money and gave it all to you. You were the money counter."

"You're a good son, Angelo. You helped us save enough money to send for Grandpa Dominic."

"Most of all, Papa, I remember you told me not to cheat anyone." Angelo smiled and got up from his chair and hugged his father.

The Schiavones' conversation remained light and friendly until suddenly everyone became quiet and Teresa started to cry. David and Samuel were confused, but Antonio explained that three years after Angelo's birth, little Mario was born. It was when the family decided to take in a boarder so that Teresa could stay home and care for him.

It was a happy time in their lives. Mario was a healthy and energetic little boy, and they felt blessed they had Grandpa with them because in 1924, the Immigration Act was passed and it would have prevented their reunion. One Sunday afternoon, tragedy struck. Little Mario ran out into the dark hallway where the rickety dark staircase was waiting. He tripped and fell to the bottom of the stairs. They heard the crash and his screams and then, silence. Mario was only three years old when he died in that wretched hall.

Teresa, Antonio, Angelo, and Dominic blamed themselves for not catching Mario before he ran into the hallway, and the grief-stricken family prayed and begged Saint Joseph for peace and a better place to live.

"God needed our little Mario," Grandpa Dominic said.

"He'll be waiting for us to be with him in heaven. God will watch over him. We'll all be together someday." Teresa said tearfully.

The first summer without Mario was bearable only because of their annual trek to the farms of southern Erie County where they worked all day and had no time to think. The family left in early spring and returned home in autumn with dark suntans and cash in their pockets, which was mainly used to pay the neighborhood grocer.

Each year before leaving for the Mustachio's Farm on Route 62 outside the town of North Collins, the family gathered together basic food supplies, including five-pound bags of flour, tuna, pepperoni, and sausage. Everything was packed in cloth bundles made from sheets.

When they first arrived at the farm, all the pickers received fresh straw for their mattresses and had to make up their beds before they did anything else. All pickers shared a kitchen with other pickers and collected water from a well with their own bucket, using a shared dipper. It was a hard life, but they had sunshine, healthy air, and beautiful farmland. The family picked peas and berries in May, strawberries and raspberries in June, and beans from June until school started again in the fall.

Samuel and David sat quietly listening to the Schiavones share their stories, and then shared their own heartbreaking tale. They all vowed to have dinner more often, and David and Samuel left feeling welcomed by their new friends in America.

CHAPTER ELEVEN

No Limitations

T he Schiavones were able to move into one of my apartments in 1937 because of the success of President Roosevelt's WPA program. Actually, it saved them all from poverty. Their good fortune began three years earlier when Teresa was hired at the Colonial Radio Company located on Rano Street in the Black Rock section of the city. She heard about the job opening from Mr. Calasandra, the neighborhood grocer. It happened when Teresa went to pay the family's bill and heard his brand-new Colonial radio playing Italian music.

"Mrs. Schiavone, how you like my new radio?" Mr. Calasandra said.

"It's beautiful. The music reminds me of being back home in Sicily."

"My daughter Nida helped build this radio and bought it for me on my birthday."

"Someday, after we save enough money to move to the West Side, I'm going to buy a used one. After I get a full-time job."

"My Nida used to be a seamstress, like you. Her hands helped her get a new job. Maybe Colonial Radio Company is hiring. I'll ask her."

The following week, Mr. Calasandra was waiting for Teresa and handed her an application. "This is for you. You're a good woman. I told Nida to ask them for an application."

"Oh! Oh! Thank you, Mr. Calasandra. Your Nida is an angel!"

Teresa was hired and became one of about twenty-one female operators at each of the main assembly lines. She added a small component as the radio chassis moved forward. She had only seconds to finish before the next component arrived, so her fingers had to be nimble to get the radio ready for tubing. Her seamstress skills made it possible for her to keep up with all the other girls.

Teresa's supervisor respected her and her strong work ethic and told her about my modest apartment building on Niagara Street and Potomac Avenue. He knew the owner had a vacant apartment for rent, and he said he would vouch for their family. Teresa was excited because it was close to her job and in a nice neighborhood. It was a dream come true, and the Schiavones were happy but sad because their little Mario wouldn't be with them.

While living in my building, the Schiavones became close friends with the Jablonski family—Stanley, his wife Sophie, and their eighteen-year-old son Wally who moved into my building later in 1937.

Originally, Stanley Jablonski, his wife, and two young daughters Alina and Anita arrived in America in 1915 along with his father Stefan and mother Stella. They came from a divided Poland ruled by three foreign powers: Russia, Prussia, and Austria. Their peasant village of Silesia, a rural area of Poland, was under Prussian control. The family was fortunate because Stanley's two older brothers and their families were already living in America and sent them the money for their entire steerage passage to America.

They also had a place to stay in their relative's crowded settlement house in the "Polish Colony" on Seneca and Exchange Streets until they could find a place of their own.

Thousands of Polish families left their homeland because of economic, political, and religious reasons, and the Jablonskis were among the first wave of Poles called *"Za chlebem"* or "For Bread" immigrants, who wanted to make money and return to their homeland. Many who came to America worked hard, saved money, and returned to Poland, only experienced more poverty and decided to return to America again. The Jablonskis wanted to stay and build a secure future for their family. They arrived in America with few possessions and only spoke Polish. They did have farming experience but little formal education. What they did have was each other and their Roman Catholic faith.

When they arrived in downtown Buffalo on the New York Central train, all their extended family were waiting for them. They were given one room—for all six of them—and the housing conditions were terrible. There was barely room to eat and sleep, and the smells were unbearable.

Stanley was able to get a job right away as a laborer working on the docks in the Canal District, and after a short period of time, he got another job in the Buffalo stockyards. It was dirty and brutal work, but it helped the family survive and save money toward an apartment of their own. Grandpa Stefan was hired to sweep streets, and then he took a job as a laborer on the docks in the Canal District. It was important to Sophie that little Alina and Anita attended school, so while everyone else was working or in school, she cared for two of someone else's babies.

When the sisters were home from school, they helped Grandma Stella with her seamstress work. Stella cooked, baked, and cleaned their tiny apartment, only the dirt in the tenement building seemed to multiply like flies in the summer heat. No space in the apartment was wasted. Every member of the family had a spot for their belongings. Their church was the only refuge from their crowded home.

Back in Poland, Grandpa Stefan made all his own furniture for their small thatched cottage. It was what he loved to do whenever he had any extra time, but now that was impossible. No one in the Jablonski family had time for anything except work. They learned fast that America's streets were not paved with gold but with sweat, blood, and tears.

When the family was able to, they moved into another tenement building on Maiden Lane where they had three small rooms instead of one. They even took in a boarder who shared half a room.

In 1916, Sophie had a miscarriage and then a stillbirth the following year. Both babies were boys, and the family was heartbroken. Three years later, Wally was born. His parents and sisters were proud because he was a first-generation Polish American, and they couldn't wait to become citizens themselves. They studied English each night after supper and registered for citizenship classes.

In 1922, tragedy struck again on a beautiful sunny afternoon after church. Grandma Stella was cooking dinner when she suddenly doubled over in pain at the dinner table. She refused to see a doctor. "I'll be better in the morning," she promised. "Let me go lie down."

After Alina and Anita cleaned the kitchen, Grandpa Stefan, Sophie, and Stanley started getting their clothes ready for work in the morning. When the girls went to check on their Grandma, they screamed for help. Only it was too late. Grandma Stella passed away, and the family would never be the same. Little Alina and Anita were only thirteen and fourteen when their Grandma Stella died. I never got used to hearing about the heartbreaks of each family. We all have them, and I can't change anyone's life. Death seems to come knocking at everyone's door. Like it or not, there is no escape when it happens, and when I hear my tenants' stories, I feel their pain and want to comfort them but can't. The Jablonskis' next ten years were filled with hard work and two small weddings. Soon the sisters had small children of their own, and their husbands, both brothers, had secure jobs. Within a few years, they were able to move into homes of their own in Black Rock—the second largest Polish section of the city in northwestern Buffalo.

Stanley was able to get a full-time job at the Bethlehem Steel Plant. It was hard labor and a dirty job, but the weekly paycheck was worth it. Their savings were growing in the Polish Savings and Loan Bank, and soon they were able to move into my building. This way they could be closer to their daughters and grandchildren.

Sophie knew Grandma Stella would have loved her new kitchen. She decorated it with matching table cloth, curtains, towels, and aprons all made from the same material in a multicolored floral print. Later, I saw Sophie with the same color blouse—I saw firsthand that the small family was frugal, like the Schiavones and Samuel and David.

Sophie learned how to make all of Stella's favorite foods, and when she cooked, my entire building smelled like Grandma Stella's homemade pierogies, apple strudel, mushroom soup, and famous duck soup. She would have been proud. She'd also be smiling to see the Easter Palm herb bouquet blessed on Assumption Day sitting right next to a small bowl of holy water.

Sophie Jablonski and Teresa Schiavone met in the summer of 1937 while tending their small vegetable gardens on the back side of my narrow lot. They began talking about their vegetables and ended up talking about their families' lives and immigrant experiences.

Soon the families shared Sunday dinners at the Schiavones and Polish holiday suppers at the Jablonskis.

Both families liked to reminisce about their summers and falls, picking crops or working in the canning factories. They each had stories to tell about being out in the fields from dawn to dusk.

When cousins David and Samuel first had dinner with the Schiavones and the Jablonskis, the two men found themselves shocked again, remembering that in Russia they could only have friendships among their own community. These families easily welcomed them into their home and made them feel accepted and special.

Late one night in 1938, David and Samuel came home from work with great news. Their mentor, Mr. Beam, used his contacts to get them both hired to work on Kleinhans Music Hall, located on Symphony Circle, a walking distance away. The project was mainly funded by the estates of Edward and Mary Kleinhans, owners of Kleinhans Men's Clothing Store, with special funds from the WPA. They couldn't wait to tell their new friends, the Schiavones and the Jablonskis, about their good fortune.

When they opened their apartment door that evening, they dropped down on their knees to say a prayer. When they stood up, they hugged and held each other close, knowing their lives were about to change. All they could think about was how they would be reunited with both of their fathers. Their goal was to soon be able to buy a two-flat home and arrange for Samuel's sisters to come to America. They knew it would be difficult to do because of the 1924 Immigration Law, but they were still hopeful.

The bad news was that the war in Europe was still raging, and all my immigrants were nervous and fearful about the families they left behind. I saw how my Jewish, Italian, and Polish families were heartbroken, fearful, and stressed about what was happening. They'd often talk quietly after supper with tears streaming down their faces. I couldn't understand why so many people all over the world were filled with hatred just because someone was different.

In 1939, David and Samuel bought their first home with a cottage in the back, and they quickly sent for both their fathers and Samuel's sisters in Russia. I'll never forget how both cousins shed tears of happiness when they purchased their first home. They both felt blessed that their fathers were still alive. It was a time of sadness too because of the loss of David's sister, Rachel, and Samuel's friend, Peril. Now both men's mothers and both sets of grandparents were deceased. But it was a dream come true to be able to send for Samuel's surviving sisters still in Russia.

It was a privilege to have David and Samuel in my building. I will miss them like I miss all my tenants. I observed, admired, and learned so much from both men. They had remarkable resilience and the will to survive. I'm only a building and have no power to make choices or solve my problems. But I do have hope, and as long as I exist, I will honor my tenants' memories in my tales.

In the Jablonski household, Grandpa Stefan was no longer able to handle a job but was still strong enough to work on making his handmade furniture a piece at a time. Young Wally was now twenty and working full-time at the Meyer Malting Grain Elevator on Niagara Street. It was the first concrete workhouse constructed in Buffalo. He was saving money to be able to move into an apartment with one of his best friends. The Jablonskis still lived with me for another year before they bought their own house, a double flat in Black Rock. The Schiavones' son, Angelo, enlisted in the army in 1941 when the United States entered World War II, and the family stayed in my building until the war ended in 1945. Thankfully,

Angelo came home safely and was accepted into the University of Buffalo using the government's first GI Bill. The Schiavones then bought themselves a large home on Connecticut Street.

Before they all moved out, I found out that David and Samuel invited the Schiavones and the Jablonskis to a special Seder dinner in their new home. Their distant cousin, Jacob, the "Notions" peddler, also bought his family a home on the same street, Lafayette Avenue, and they were neighbors at last. America was now their official homeland, and they vowed to never leave their new country. Jacob opened a small used furniture shop on Niagara Street, and both cousins' fathers worked in the shop helping Grandpa Stefan Jablonski create his handmade furniture. All three families were now one big family. I've had many families live in my building, but it's hard for me to let them go. I've protected all of my tenants within my walls and enabled them to earn their wings and fly away like the baby birds who nested in my trees.

Learning about different cultures and ethnicities taught me that freedom isn't free at all but comes with a heavy price. My diverse families shared their stories and differences with each other. Although they were different, they were filled with heartaches, struggles, and hope for the future.

My strength lies in my ability to have the time to think and reflect on all I see, hear, and witness. Sometimes it's hard, and I struggle trying to make sense of my life. All I can do is to live vicariously through my tenants' lives. What they all wanted most was to escape from wars, poverty, and political oppression. They wanted opportunities to work to support their families, have a home of their own, and an education for their children and their children's children.

My tenants loved having freedom in America and grew roots of resiliency for future generations to come. I witnessed in real time how cultural differences and understanding can turn strangers into friends.

CHAPTER TWELVE

. . . .

Orphan Train Rider Tales

It was a Sunday afternoon in 1938 when I first heard Benedict Farley, Benny for short, running up the stairs to one of my third-floor apartments. He didn't have much furniture to carry, but he was with my beautiful suffragette Kathleen Duffy. I saw her follow him slowly up the stairs while she kept turning her head backward toward the bottom of the landing as though she was looking for someone.

In my mind's eye, I thought Kathleen was thinking of her youthful life here in my building. If I could only talk to her and tell her how much I missed her spirit and courage. All I could do was embrace the sight of her helping Benny up the stairs.

Benedict was born in New York City in 1913. He was the child of Beth and her husband, William Farley. He was only a year old when his father abandoned them both to be with another woman. One evening when Benny was five, his mother suddenly became ill at work. She had a fever, then chills, and finally passed out on the floor while cleaning rooms. An ambulance was called, but Benny's mum died in the emergency room.

When Beth's neighbor "Auntie Sarah," Benny's babysitter, opened the door, a policeman stood there with his hat in his hand. "I'm sorry, Ma'am, I have bad news. Mrs. Beth Farley has died, and Miss

Sharon, a social worker, is here to take her little boy to the Brooklyn Industrial School Association and Home for Destitute Children."

Auntie Sarah and Benny both cried when the "black hat" lady took him out of her arms.

The only thing Benny remembered about his Mum was how much he loved and missed her every day.

When he was eight years old, he was taken to his first foster home. He stayed there until he ran away on his eleventh birthday because of the abusive treatment from his foster parents.

Living on the streets of New York City wasn't easy, either. Benny was constantly afraid of being caught and taken back to his foster home. What he missed most was going to school. After a month of his being on the streets, the cops found him digging in garbage cans and took him to the station house. At first, Benny wouldn't talk. When they asked about his family, he said, "I don't have one."

They checked the missing children's file and found his picture among others from the Home for Destitute Children and immediately contacted them. Benny was returned to the orphanage, which was a safer place than the foster home he was placed in.

In 1926, when Benny was thirteen, he became part of a mass migration of thousands of children sent on orphan trains out to the Midwest to join farm families. The Orphan Train Program existed from 1853 to 1929 and was formed by Charles Loring Brace and a group of social reformers, who also founded the Children's Aid Society (CAS). Benny was placed on a train with twenty other children and was told only that he was taking a long train ride. Benny was scared and didn't trust anyone. Most of the children on the train were from the same orphanage and were between the ages of five and thirteen. They were supervised by Miss Hammond, a western agent from the Children's Aid Society. Benny always remembered her name because she was kind to him.

At each train stop, they had to make sure they were clean and dressed properly. Their hair had to be combed, and they had to use their best manners because the screening committee would be meeting them at the train station. Miss Hammond kept telling the children how lucky they were to be going to new families. Benny was one of the older boys who wanted to run away when they found out what was happening. They watched carefully as the committee made up of important community members and local families told them to stand in a straight line. The committee issued a special paper for the kids who were selected that allowed them to be placed with their new families. Benny felt like they were being sold. Miss Hammond promised the older kids that they could go to school until they were eighteen if they were selected. Most of the older boys, including Benny, were tall and sturdy and would be able to lift heavy bales of hay and do additional farm work.

"They'll treat you like their own family," Miss Hammond promised. "Maybe they'll even adopt you. All you have to do is try your best and write to me regularly. The head of your new family will write to me once a year unless there are problems and they want to send you back."

Benny's farm family of five was from Missouri. The head of the family poked and examined him before he was picked to live with them. They had three daughters and no boys. All he did was work, and he wasn't allowed any contact with his new sisters unless it was in the presence of their mother and father. In less than a month, Benny made sure he got in trouble by answering the father back and slacking off on his farmwork so that he would be sent back to the orphanage in New York City.

In 1927, when Benny was fourteen, his caseworker tried one more time to help him by sending him to Bowdoin Farm School for training in Hamburg, New York. It was his only chance to get a job. At Bowdoin Farm School, he was treated fairly and learned to be an excellent farm laborer. He was almost seventeen when the school stopped taking new boys because it was scheduled to close as soon as the Orphan Train Program ended. Benny was fortunate because he was hired as a farm laborer at Weiss Farms in Eden, New York.

The Children's Aid Society continued to track all the Orphan Train riders, and Benny's Buffalo field agent, Kathleen Duffy, was responsible for making regular visits to the school. When I heard this, I wondered if this happened by chance or was it by fate? Actually, she was responsible for checking on all three of the orphan train riders who were hired from their orphanage in New York City. In 1930, when Benny turned seventeen and Kathleen's last report was finished, she invited him to visit the city of Buffalo, her hometown.

That visit changed Benny's life forever.

Kathleen invited him to her apartment for lunch and fed him her homemade chicken soup and chocolate cake. No one had ever done something special for him before. Then, she did something extraordinary that shocked Benny by offering to rent him her second bedroom in the apartment. This would give him time to save money to get a place of his own because the depression raged on and jobs were scarce. Kathleen also arranged for Benny to have an apprenticeship in her brother-in-law's insurance business. I saw how Kathleen worried about him. It was the first time he felt loved and respected, except for before his mum died. When I heard what happened, it made me happy. I knew we were both lucky to have Kathleen in our lives.

Fast forward to 1937 when twenty-four-year-old Benny was hired at the Ford Plant where he could save enough money to afford to rent his own apartment, plus accumulate a savings account with a healthy balance. He considered it one of the best years of his life.

One evening, Kathleen came home late from work with exciting news. "Benny, I found you an apartment in a nice neighborhood, with a bus stop right on the corner, and it has affordable rent," Kathleen said excitedly. "The Skyway Tavern is right across the street, and they have homemade food."

"Kathleen, let's go see it now! I'll buy some used furniture, a bed, couch, and kitchen table! I can't thank you enough."

Benny seemed genuinely excited, but he became suddenly quiet.

"What's wrong, Benny?"

"Kathleen, today I found out why my Mum named me Benedict."

"Why?"

"All my life I've been teased about my name. It's not Irish. In the orphanage, I was called Benedict Arnold by the older boys. I never knew who he was until I was about sixteen when my teacher told me he was an American traitor who lived during the Revolutionary period. But now I've found out the real reason I was named Benedict.

"Well, I met a man at the Ford Plant. His name is Salvatore Verdi; he's Sicilian, and his father's name is Benedict, and he was named after one of the sixteen popes. Then, he told me that Benedict means blessed. Salvatore told me that Saint Benedict was an Italian monk who founded the Benedictines in the sixth century and then he said that the name was even popular in England in the twelfth century. I couldn't believe it. I've decided I no longer want to be called Benny. From now on, I'm going to be proud of my name."

"Benedict, your time has come. Your mum knew what she was doing when she named you. She wanted you to be strong and honorable. You're a blessing to her memory." This was good news to me too. I'd just found out how important a name can be. I think my name, Fred, is a common name, like me. I'm not pretentious. I'm finding out what it's like to be alive in the twentieth century and telling tales of my own.

CHAPTER THIRTEEN

· · · · · · · · · · · · · · · · · ·

Building a Future

In 1938, Bianca Martucci moved into my second-floor apartment. It was the same day Anna moved in right next door to her. Needless to say, my narrow hall was extremely busy, and I couldn't wait to get to know them.

The next day, Anna brought two bowls of beef stew over to Bianca's apartment as a token of friendship.

"We're neighbors now," she said, smiling. "I love to cook and share my food."

"Oh, it smells delicious!" Bianca replied. "Please come in, only I haven't settled in yet."

"It's okay, Bianca. I'm here to meet you, not your furniture."

It was fun to find out about my personable Bianca and Anna—a stately, widowed middle-aged elementary teacher from New London, Connecticut. In the beginning, they would have supper together on Sunday afternoons in Anna's apartment. Bianca would make sure to bring something sweet or some kind of meat to help pay for the cost of her dinner.

I learned that she was orphaned in 1926 at seven years old. Her mom died in a freak accident on her way home from her afternoon cleaning job at the Hotel Worth downtown in the city. Her mom tripped and fell, hitting her head on the street's curb, and passed away on the way to the hospital from concussion complications. Rose Barker, her good friend, took care of little Bianca until the family priest, Father Jim Sarach, took her to the Saint Vincent's Female Orphan Asylum in Buffalo. At the time, Bianca was one of 283 children in Buffalo who were provided with a foster home by the Children's Aid Society.

"Anna, all I can remember is that my momma never came home from work. I kept waiting for her to come take me away from the orphanage. Then, my babysitter told me that she went to heaven and the orphanage was going to be my new home."

Nine-year-old Bianca had never had a female friend before except for Miss Mary Zablocki—a nurse at the orphanage. Miss Mary was gentle with her when she was returned to the orphanage after being beaten by her foster father and removed from her first and only foster home placement in 1929.

"Anna, Miss Mary was my best friend. She hugged me whenever I saw her and told me I was special. Sometimes I even faked being sick, so I could see her. I decided way back then that someday I would become a nurse and help others like she helped me to heal on the outside and inside. Miss Mary taught me to never give up. Someday I hope I can find her and let her know how she saved me."

"Bianca, you turned into a wonderful young woman, and I think we will become great friends."

"I was happy to be sent back to the Saint Vincent DePaul Orphanage. We lived in groups to resemble a large family. We had a furnished living room, our own beds, and sleeping quarters. The goal was to help us become educated young women who were both spiritual and self-sufficient. Depending on our ages, we had household duties before school. We attended school from 9:00 a.m.

to 3:00 p.m., including a half-hour recreation break every day. We were up at 6:00 a.m. and to bed by 8:00 p.m. There were never any visitors and no overnight visits were allowed. Sometimes, late at night, I'd dream about talking to my momma and papa."

"Honey, I'm sorry you lost your parents so young. It must have been terrible."

Then, I saw both women cry. It's when I found out that Bianca's own mother became a World War I widow shortly after her father enlisted in the army six months before she was born. Her papa promised her mother that he would come home safe and sound, but he didn't, and her mother never stopped grieving for him.

"I'm so sorry, Anna, Bianca said. We have a lot in common, and I'm glad we're friends."

When Bianca was fourteen, she took sewing classes at the Saint Vincent's Dress Making School. It wasn't only for orphans but also for local girls who wanted to make dressmaking an occupation; their specialties included wedding gowns, baptismal dresses, and burial robes, as well as table linens, gowns, and trousseaus. The school's excellent reputation kept the seamstresses in demand for Buffalo's wealthy socialites.

Listening to Bianca tell Anna about her life revealed a strong woman. "I was a seamstress when I left the orphanage at eighteen and ended up as a boarder in one of my private client's carriage houses on the West Side. But I always wanted an apartment of my own, so I found a second job as a waitress at the Skyway Tavern. The extra tips I earn helped me to save money to rent this apartment."

Anna Good was born in 1897. Up until that time, I didn't know anything about stoic New Englanders. Only it didn't take long for me to see strength and fortitude in my new tenant. Anna considered herself to be a "Swamp Yankee," a term sometimes used to describe

Northeastern farmers who emigrated from England. It must have been why Anna carried herself proudly, with the same determination and self-sufficiency as her ancestors.

Anna married her husband Jack right after high school graduation. He was a construction and maintenance worker at the New London Naval Academy. In 1917, he was drafted into World War I. Anna was pregnant when he left, but six months later, she lost the baby girl in a miscarriage, and it was the same year her papa died of influenza. Anna's mother died four months later of bronchitis and a broken heart. Then, the unthinkable happened. Jack was mortally wounded in the summer of 1918 in the Battle of Amiens on the Seine River in northwestern France.

Anna told Bianca she was married, pregnant, and widowed within the same year.

"I'm sorry, Anna. How did you cope?"

"The same way you did, dear. By putting one foot in front of the other. What else could I do? I knew my parents and my husband loved me and believed in me. I had to find a way to give my life meaning again. I love children and what better way to be a part of a child's life than to teach? Teaching saved me from a life of self-pity."

I have to tell you how often grief arrived uninvited into all my tenants' lives. I wished I could make this part of their lives disappear, but my tales have to be realistic. Witnessing the pain they experienced made me stronger and wiser. My Anna experienced a triple tragedy. It was terrible to hear, and how she managed to cope and get through her losses was beyond belief. I remember thinking how brave she was to rebuild her life without her loved ones by her side.

She taught elementary school from 1924 to 1936 and came to Buffalo because her mother's only living relative, her Aunt Carrie, needed help. She was a retired school teacher in her late seventies who lived in a small apartment on the West Side of Buffalo, not far from my building.

Aunt Carrie died suddenly in late 1937, and Anna had to move out of the apartment. Their next-door neighbor told her about my empty apartment soon after she was hired as a teacher at School #3 on Niagara Street.

I was surprised to find out that Benedict often stopped at the Skyway Tavern on his way home from working the late shift. He'd have a sandwich and a beer before going home, and Bianca told Anna he was polite and left her a generous tip.

She never ever had a boyfriend and only dreamed of someday meeting the love of her life—but there was something special about this young man she could not deny. Benedict told Anna he lived right across the street. "I told him I did too. Then, he asked me if I had a boyfriend. I felt flushed and shook my head no. Then, he asked me if I'd like to go to the movies with him, and I said yes." Bianca told Anna.

That moment was the beginning of many movie dates and long walks in the neighborhood. They even had their first kiss in my second-floor hallway!

Within a few weeks, Anna, Benedict, and Bianca were all sharing Sunday dinners together. I remember how Anna's childhood stories entertained us. They made me laugh, want to cry, and think about her extraordinary life.

"My father owned a successful plumbing and heating business and worked hard and had a quick temper, but it went away just as quickly. He swore a lot, usually in French, but he didn't use "f" or "b" words—mostly just Jesus H. Connecticut Christ. It was when I knew he was really angry. I never ever found out what the letter *H* stood for. But I did learn to say French words!"

Anna loved to tell stories about the people that lived in the town where she grew up. One evening, she told us about New London, a small place with hills everywhere. She told us she walked them all. When I say us, I mean me too.

Her favorite place, though, was Ye Olde Town Mill built by John Winthrop, a wealthy English Puritan lawyer and one of the important figures among the Puritan founders of New England in the 1600s.

We learned about Nathan Hale, who was a soldier who fought in the Continental Army during the American Revolutionary War. I wanted to ask Anna questions about Nathan Hale's family, but I couldn't. Only I did find out when she explained that Nathan had volunteered for an intelligence-gathering mission in New York City, only to be captured by the British and executed. I learned that there was a lot of history in New London, Connecticut; especially in the early nineteenth century, New London was the world's third busiest whaling port after New Bedford and Nantucket. Plus, the city had the Thames River on one side and the Atlantic Ocean on the other.

Anna was excited when she told us about Boat Race Day, her favorite time of the year. Everyone celebrated and many people traveled from nearby states to see all the competition. The Harvard and Yale rowing crews would race on the Thames River—red for Harvard and blue for Yale. Her father and brother Jackie wore red (her father was originally from Massachusetts), and the rest of her family wore blue. There were so many yachts on the river that it was difficult to see the boats in the race. She also recalled the excursion train with long benches and canvas tops that were used to protect riders from the sun as the train ran alongside the river. Anna's grandfather was also the conductor who drove that train.

We found out that celebrities and vendors of all kinds were in the park and on the surrounding streets. Her front porch was just a hundred feet from the grounds, so she could see everything from there. But Anna agreed that it was more fun being among the crowds wearing her pretty blue dress. Everybody was in a festive mood, she said, mainly because it was a chance to spend the entire day with her father. He treated her special, and when he was home, he protected her from an overbearing mother, who favored her two brothers. How she wished Boat Race Day happened more than once a year.

Suddenly, she took a deep breath and looked sadly at Bianca with tears in her eyes. "My father worked extremely hard, and I didn't see him often enough. I remember how I'd often 'plug' up the toilet with all manner of things to get him to come home from work. Once I even used a small potato to block it.

"When my dad came home to fix the toilet, I'd sit on the floor and talk to him, then other times, I'd sit at the dining room table and help him figure out the price of materials and expenses for a plumbing job. Usually, it happened when everybody else would be asleep in the house, except for me and my daddy.

"Sometimes me, my mom, and my cousin Mary would take a ride on Grandpa's train. During his layover, we stayed in his hotel room where he told us to be very quiet and introduced us to his friends—he called them Tim and Dave. All of a sudden, two mice came out of a hole in the wall, climbed up on Grandpa's knees, and he fed them cheese. Later, he clapped his hands, and they went back into the hole! We laughed so hard, we had tears in our eyes."

Boy, Anna sure loved to tell her stories.

When I saw Benedict and Bianca alone together, I saw how they respected each other and were happy they were now a couple. I knew they were falling in love with each other. It was good to see them have fun together and enjoy each other's company.

It was the year Benedict, Bianca, and Anna all became best friends. By 1939, Benny and Bianca were inseparable, and Anna was like a mom to both of them.

CHAPTER FOURTEEN

· · · · · · · · · · · · · · · · · · · ·

World War II: Death Comes Knocking

I t happened the night Benny and Bianca were at the Marlowe Theater, sometimes called the "Scratch House," watching *How Green Was My Valley*. It was December 7, 1941, when suddenly the movie stopped, and the lights came on. An army officer walked onto the stage and spoke, "The Japanese Army has bombed Pearl Harbor. All servicemen return to your base immediately."

"At first we were in shock, and then there was dead silence. No one moved from their seats. We both realized it was only a matter of time before he would be drafted. Right then and there, Benny asked me to marry him as soon as possible, and I said yes." Bianca told Anna.

"Bianca, I know you both are doing the right thing. You love each other, and if it were me, I'd get married too." Anna said.

When I heard their conversation, I was happy too. But deep down, I wanted to share my life with someone too. On the other hand, by thinking positively, I can observe, think, and feel my tenants' emotions most of the time. Meanwhile, I'm beginning to find out what it feels like to be contented with what I can do, not what I can't.

A week later, they were married by a justice of the peace. Everyone in the building came to Anna's apartment for coffee and cake, and Benny gave his notice to the landlord that he would be giving up his apartment to move in with his wife Bianca immediately.

It wasn't long before he was drafted into the army. Bianca took the trip with him to the New York Central Terminal to say goodbye. They were not alone. Hundreds of young men were also there saying goodbyes to their wives, girlfriends, children, and extended families.

When Bianca arrived home, she found Anna crying, and they both shed more tears together because they were afraid of what might happen to their treasured Benny.

The following month, Bianca found out she was pregnant and wrote to her husband immediately. "My dear husband, Benny, I'm going to have our baby. Yes, you are going to be a father! A wonderful father! I'm hoping he will be a boy named Benedict Jr. He'll be born around the middle of October, and I pray you stay safe and come home to us. We missed having our own families growing up, but our baby will have a family filled with all the love we lost."

During World War II, Bianca used the military V-mail, which was limited to one piece of paper about the size of a writing tablet. The letters also had to be folded into an official envelope because they were read and copied before soldiers received them.

Bianca sent many tear-stained letters to her husband, and Anna wrote to Benny reassuring him that Bianca and the growing baby were doing well. Both women put together care packages for him to share with his fellow servicemen, but most of all, they prayed for his safety and the war to end.

Listening to the radio, I learned how women were involved in all aspects of the war industry. Working both day and night, they did everything from making military clothing to building fighter jets. Women of all ages were hired to operate large cranes used to move heavy tanks or work as welders, riveters, drill press operators, and taxi cab drivers, as well as volunteer firefighters. They did everything they could for the war effort. These women were called "Production Soldiers."

Bianca was hired at General Motors, the same plant where Benedict had worked. She was hired the same month she found out she was expecting a baby. She worked forty-eight hours a week and saved all she could to provide for her growing family.

Anna continued to teach and volunteer every weekend for the Red Cross, whose mission was to assist and support President Roosevelt's New Deal Program. Because of the war, Roosevelt's program moved away from domestic social issues and toward international concerns while the U.S. economy expanded to support the war effort. Thousands of plants exported supplies, including 2.5 million trucks, and 50 million pairs of shoes.

The U.S. Government rationed basic foods like sugar, milk, cheese, butter, coffee, eggs, meat, and canned goods because of the difficulty of getting farmer's goods to the market. I couldn't believe what was happening outside my walls and in the world. But things were changing inside my building, too. Tenants began planting small individual vegetable gardens and shared their vegetables and various fruits with all the tenants. When all the dirt was gone, they formed an unofficial dirt patrol. My tenants were constantly on the lookout for any unsupervised pile of dirt, large or small, that they could take home night or day.

I started to notice that all empty containers large enough to hold a plant were used to increase the crops. I even saw neighborhood kids taking my tenants' ripe fruits and vegetables in the middle of the night. I couldn't tell on them—even if I could talk—because I knew everyone was hungry for fresh food, especially for our delicious tomatoes.

While the war was being fought, our government put out a new product, a butter substitute that everyone complained about, but there was nothing anyone could do. It was a block that looked like what they called lard, with a button in the middle. You pressed on it, and it released a yellow dye. Then, you kept squeezing it until it was formed into a shape resembling butter. Bianca and Anna said it tasted terrible.

During the war years, everyone had a story to tell. No one ever complained for too long, though, because we were fighting a war. Bianca, Anna, and my other tenants knew it was a small sacrifice to make when our men and women were dying overseas.

The prayers I heard during those years still echo in my mind. Each tenant felt the pain of war because everyone knew someone fighting in World War II. I saw their tears, felt their anger, frustration, and panic whenever they heard the radio describe the latest war casualties or when they read the latest newspaper headlines. I wanted to help them, but of course, I couldn't. It reminded me of World War I, when my twin suffragettes, Patricia and Kathleen, lived in the building. Any knock on any door was gut-wrenching, and I could always hear a sigh of relief when it wasn't bad news. Now it was the same response and fear about who was behind every unopened door. I asked myself, "Why? Why do people fight and kill people who also have families, friends, and leave broken hearts at home?" I'm a building learning a lot about what happens in one's lifetime.

On October 16, 1942, Benedict Jr. was born, and Anna stayed with Bianca so she wouldn't be alone with the love of her life. They were overjoyed when they saw the baby.

"Honey," Anna said, "your baby has a daddy who loves him more than life itself."

When Bianca signed her son's birth certificate, she named him Benedict Farley Jr. and decided to call him BJ for short, at least until he was old enough to understand the meaning of his name.

Since Anna never had a family of her own, she could afford to help Bianca take care of BJ. It was hard for her to see her friend struggling without her husband. It brought back memories of her own heartache when her husband was killed in World War I in the battle on the Western Front. I heard her pray for Benedict every night. Then, she filled in all her free time doing volunteer work—helping the Red Cross in the war effort to aid the military and their families. Anna was like a mother to Bianca and Benedict and a grandmother to little BJ. They could have been the children she never had, and it gave Anna a new purpose in life.

Bianca wrote to Benny every day to tell him how BJ was doing. The two women would put together care packages for him weekly and pray he'd make it home safely. On one occasion, they included one of BJ's baby blankets carefully wrapped so that he could smell the scent of his son. Bianca sent pictures of the baby as often as she could and told him how much she loved and missed him.

One horrible day, the dreaded Western Union telegram arrived. It was on January 16, 1943. BJ was three months old when Bianca's world collapsed. The only man she had ever loved was killed in the last major German offensive on the Western Front. It happened when Benedict's newly arrived 106th Infantry Division was caught in a surprise attack during heavy snowstorms that hit the battlefield in Schnee Eifel, in the Ardennes Forest, in Belgium. His division was surrounded and cut off from other American units and suffered great casualties.

Bianca could do nothing but sit on her couch, numb, waiting for Anna and BJ to return from the grocery store. When I witnessed Bianca get the news about Benedict, I wanted to reach out and hold her tightly. I wanted to tell her everything would be okay, even though I knew it wouldn't be. There was nothing I could do except watch her feel the pain of the loss of her husband and father to little BJ. Words cannot describe the depth of my sorrow in that moment. It was beyond description.

When Anna came home with BJ, Bianca grabbed the baby, scaring him with her desperate hug and wrenching sobs. The telegraph lay crumpled on the floor, but Anna didn't have to pick it up to know what it said. She reached out and held Bianca and BJ tightly in her arms. It was a moment I'll never forget. It wasn't long before everyone in the building came to pay their respect to Bianca and BJ. The tenants brought small gifts of food and money, including a wooden baby carriage. But whenever Bianca took the baby for a walk in the carriage, the wooden wheels would crack when she went up and down a curb. It got so dangerous that she couldn't use it at all. A neighbor living in the house next door always let her borrow hers when she wasn't using it until Bianca could afford to buy another one that was safer.

A blue star banner hung in Bianca's living room window before Benedict was killed, but now there was a gold star for Benedict's loss of life during the war.

I often wonder why Benedict had to die. I was angry and heartbroken. The truth is that death does not wait for an invitation to knock on our doors.

CHAPTER FIFTEEN

• • • • • • • • • • • • • • • • •

My Patch Quilt Family

B ianca continued working the day shift at General Motors, and Anna promised to continue caring for BJ until he started school. Then, Anna planned to return to teaching.

In March of 1943, Bianca came home from work excited because she found out about the Bolton Act. The act was sponsored by Frances Pane Bolton who was the first Congresswoman to be elected in the state of Ohio after her husband died in office in 1939.

Mrs. Bolton was born in 1885, and when she was a young woman, she volunteered with the Visiting Nurses Association. Frances accompanied nurses on their rounds in the poor neighborhoods of Cleveland, Ohio, but never forgot how the nurses were treated without respect. To Mrs. Bolton "nurses were the individuals who brought light, easement, intelligence, and understanding where there was darkness."

The Bolton Act was the most significant nursing legislation passed during the war years. It introduced the nation's first U.S. Nurse Cadet Corp. and would be the only federally subsidized educational program in U.S. history. It ensured that the government would have enough nurses both at home and overseas during World War II, and it also helped elevate the profession for women. Bianca believed this would give her a chance to become a nurse and support her son.

"I want you to apply," Anna told Bianca, immediately. "I'll take care of BJ until he starts kindergarten. I have money saved to help buy a house for all of us. You're my family, and I love you both. Benny would be happy for all of us."

Bianca applied and was accepted into the program. She received a scholarship, monthly stipend, and payment of all other educational fees, including the cost of her books and uniforms, in exchange for thirty months of service in the military or essential civilian nursing throughout the war. She thanked God every day that she was within the age limit of 17–35 years of age, in good health, and had graduated from high school with good grades. In her heart, she knew Benny was smiling down upon her.

For the first nine months, she was called a "probie." Then, in the next twenty-one months, she was a junior cadet and would serve and learn at the Sisters of Charity Hospital School of Nursing. Bianca loved every minute of her training, and in 1945, she became one of the 85 percent of all nursing students to enter the Cadet Nurse Corp. She was on her way to securing a sound future for herself and her son.

I watched their progress. I knew they were happy to have each other in their lives, but I wished that they could know how happy I was to have them in mine.

On September 4, 1944, at about 11:39 p.m., my building shook from top to bottom, and I thought I'd come crashing down. My tenants' walls were shaking, and everything hanging on the walls either crashed to the floor or hung crookedly. Everyone ran out onto the street. We thought we were being attacked. For a moment,

I wondered about Benedict being killed in the war. I wondered if he had the time to feel the fear of impending death.

The shaking only lasted for a few seconds. But when it stopped, I found out that what we felt was a huge tremor from an earthquake centered in Eastern Ontario, Canada. Why I immediately thought about Benedict's death, I'll never know. But it's when I realized how priceless life is, and the thoughts of Bianca, BJ, and Anna's life without him must have felt unbearable. I thought about my own existence and purpose in life and how I provide shelter and comfort to my tenants. To me, the tremor was a reminder that my existence is totally out of my hands. My sole purpose in life is to share my tenants' stories before it's too late.

Bianca's fear for Benny's safety turned into a lifetime loss of a man she loved, leaving behind a fatherless child. My moments of shaking were no comparison to her loss. Only it did give me pause about what impending death might feel like, and I'll never forget it. It made me admire Bianca more. She was determined to rebuild her life and support her son with help from Anna, who also experienced the loss of her husband in World War I. Bianca was resilient, and in late September 1945, she graduated as a member of the U.S. Nursing Cadet Corp. She was hired at Sisters of Charity Hospital where she completed her training. Everyone in the building was excited and happy for her, and they surprised her with a large cake and ice cream.

On October 16, 1945, BJ's third birthday, the war was finally over. Benny had been one of 2,261 soldiers and sailors from Erie County, New York, killed in World War II.

By 1947, Bianca and Anna had finally saved enough money for a down payment on a small house on Fargo Avenue only a short distance away. It even had a small fenced yard for BJ to play in.

I was sad when I found out that they would be moving out and into their own home in the neighborhood. I hoped that maybe someday they would come back and visit me and show BJ where he lived as a baby. When Benedict died, I worried that Bianca's hopes and dreams died with him. I'm glad she survived and thrived. I was excited to see this new family achieve their goals but sad to say goodbye. As I age, I realize I will constantly be in transition. I must accept the fact that all my tenants will move out someday. It's an integral part of my life. I'm a stopover on their way to achieving their goals. How lucky I am that most of my tenants give me an inside view of what it's like to be human. My tales are valuable because I'm the only witness to my tenants' trials, tribulations, and successes.

It is important to tell you a little more about the last story Anna shared with Bianca the night before they moved out of their apartment. It was about her great great grandpa. He lived in New Hampshire and owned a working homestead farm that dated back to the Civil War. He was her great-great-grandfather and was a Civil War veteran who fought for the Union Army in many important battles between the North and the South.

"My great-great-grandpa Good received land and a small Civil War pension for his service. This valuable land became a homestead to generations of relatives and left behind the legacy of a life well-lived. Without him, I wouldn't exist."

Anna's story struck me to my core because, unfortunately, wars seem to be a part of my tenants' lives. My building holds mountains of grief and heartache, and I listen and wonder why peace in the world is so hard to achieve outside the walls of my apartment building.

Over the decades, I've learned that wars never end and that human beings fight for land, freedom, and peace. They hope and pray their families and future generations will have a better life.

Because of war, my Benedict will never be able to raise the family he didn't have growing up. Bianca and BJ were left to fend for themselves, but thankfully, Anna's friendship became the glue that helped them all stay strong. This new "patch quilt" family meshed together by heart-wrenching circumstances would provide a safe and comforting home for BJ and a positive future for themselves. I am proud to have had them all live in my building.

Bianca, Anna, and BJ became a "patch quilt" family. Bianca and BJ moved into Anna's apartment to save money and make it easier to watch him. Then, Anna took in another child, while the mother worked. Her goal was to also return to teaching when BJ entered kindergarten.

Delicatessen located at 1469 Niagara Street, August 8, 1951.
Collection of The Buffalo History Museum.
General photograph collection, Streets – Niagara.

CHAPTER SIXTEEN

· · · · · · · · · · · · · · · · · ·

Bobby Mooney and the Chocolate Ladies

From 1947 to 1951, my life was stressful, especially when my favorite tenants—like Bianca, Anna, and BJ—moved out. During this period of time, all my apartments were rented, but for some reason, I couldn't connect with any of the tenants like I did before.

I was concerned I'd never be able to connect with another tenant again. It was a feeling I'll never forget. It was a feeling of emptiness. Usually, I connected with most of the tenant families when they first moved into their apartments. Unfortunately, up to now, no one ever knew how much I learned and cared about them.

To complicate matters, I was sold again, but I did get new plumbing and wiring, only my biggest fear was that I'd stop learning what it was like to be alive or that I'd no longer be able to live through my tenants' lives.

Toward the end of 1950, I decided I'd had enough of feeling bad. I was sick of being scared, feeling alone, and being afraid. I decided to be positive and hope for the best. After all, it was a year later and the tenants I still had left were too busy working to give me a chance to get to know them.

Now I had three of my apartments empty. I waited and watched, hoping for new tenants and their families to move in. At last, a miracle happened when ten-year-old Bobby Mooney moved into one of my second-floor apartments with his first-generation Irish mother and father, Becca and Jimmy, and his two older brothers, Billy (eleven) and Brian (twelve), and his infant sister Becky.

Right away, I noticed Bobby immediately as he trailed along behind his family when they carried their belongings up the stairs. He was a frail little boy with huge brown eyes who struggled with a large box almost as big as he was.

His father was tall, lanky, and loud, and his mother looked tired as she carried little Becky and some small boxes up the stairs. His brothers Billy and Brian laughed and joked with each other, mostly ignoring their little brother. The family's belongings came in waves in a neighbor's old red truck. No one paid much attention to Bobby, and I wondered why.

The Mooney family knew the apartment was too small for them, but it was only five minutes away from Jimmy's new job at F.N. Burt Company Box Factory—the largest manufacturer of small paper boxes in the world. Jimmy would again be able to support his family, and Becca hoped her husband would drink less and stop playing cards.

The older boys each had a cot in the second bedroom, but Bobby was told to put together a makeshift bed in the bedroom's tiny closet. His bed consisted of three old blankets folded lengthwise and a pillow, but his feet stuck out past the open closet door. Sometimes when his brothers were out of the house, Bobby would stretch out on one of their cots and imagine what it would be like to have a bed of his own.

He hardly ever caused his mother any problems, so there was no reason to give him any extra attention. His brothers kept bothering his mother until they got what they wanted, and she always doted on little Becky. Quiet Bobby became the "gofer" for the family.

"Do this, Bobby—get my, hold this, fix this." That was how they spoke to him.

"Ma, can I have a kiss, too? Like Becky?" Bobby would plead.

"You're too big, Bobby," she would answer. That's the way it was for Bobby Mooney.

I learned the most about their family on the nights Jimmy got drunk sitting at the kitchen table having beers with the same neighbor who'd helped them move in. Both men would talk about the good old days in 1939 when the Mooneys moved into their first small home on Myrtle Avenue.

Jimmy was able to get a good job as a factory worker at the Bethlehem Steel Plant in Lackawanna in 1934 when he was eighteen years old. It was a dirty job, but he made a decent wage, and it allowed him to afford the down payment on their first home.

Life changed abruptly when the U.S. entered World War II in 1941. Within a year, Jimmy Mooney was drafted into the army, leaving his young family behind. Becca wrote to him faithfully via V-mail, but in 1944, Jimmy was honorably discharged from the military because of "trench foot" and dysentery. He was injured when he was in Northern France during the Battle of Normandy, which began on June 6, 1944, and lasted until dawn on June 30, 1944, when the Allies invaded Western Europe in the largest amphibious attack in history.

Jimmy was one of 156,000 Allied troops who stormed Normandy's beaches on D-Day. The troops had to live outdoors in trenches; their feet were soaked, never able to dry, and exposed to constant cold weather. The weather destroyed the skin on his feet and affected his circulation. His feet developed a grayish color, felt numb, heavy, painful, and prickly. Jimmy came home from the war with a 50 percent disability with rotting feet that smelled horrible. He had to wear white socks for the rest of his life. On top of all of Jimmy's problems, he developed anemia, causing him to often feel tired and weak.

Because of his new health problems, Jimmy lost his job at the steel plant. When his feet got better, he had to find an easier job, one where he wouldn't be exposed to constant cold and damp conditions. To complicate matters, the couple struggled to afford to pay the mortgage on their house. Becca started working a part-time evening job cleaning the Buffalo Savings Bank on Main Street in Downtown Buffalo.

Everything went downhill when their house went into foreclosure. Becca had to give up her job and continue to care for her growing family. Jimmy wanted desperately to support them and finally landed a job at the F.N. Burt Company Box Factory and found an apartment in my building, which was almost directly across the street from the box factory.

I watched Bobby's disjointed family and saw how they were different from my other families. Maybe it was because the Mooneys' marriage took a turn for the worse when Jimmy was drafted and returned home with a serious disability. Or maybe it was because when Jimmy lost his job at the steel plant, he felt like a failure and drank too much.

Jimmy was raised to be tough. He had to be because nothing was ever given to his parents or any of his grandparents. They had to fight to survive their poverty. In Ireland, his family was always controlled by others. Being poor, hungry, and unemployed made physical and mental toughness an asset.

Listening to Jimmy talk about the past with his friend was an eye-opener. He was a proud Irishman, and both his parents came to Buffalo in 1910 directly from Ellis Island. They settled in the Old First Ward, and his father, Patrick, worked on the Erie Canal, scooped grain from ships, and helped build railroads. "We Irish are tough!" his father would say to him growing up. "Ain't no one gonna beat us down."

Over time, especially on the weekends, a few of Jimmy's army veteran friends would come to visit. The kitchen table served as their "watering hole." They drank beer, played cards, and talked about how life used to be before the war. Little Bobby would often sit silently on the floor in a corner of the kitchen and listen. The older boys now worked as newsboys before and after school since their family still needed the extra money because Jimmy's pay didn't cover all their expenses.

Bobby was shy and withdrawn. He often heard his ma and pa argue every time he lost money playing cards.

"Ma, why is Pa yelling?" Bobby would ask.

"You never mind," she'd answer, wiping tears from her cheeks. "Go play." Then, off he'd go to find a quiet spot alone in the farthest corner of their sparse living room.

Bobby's ma had a tough family history, too. "The men ruled the roost," she said to her new next-door neighbor, twenty-five-year-old Hannah. "My ma taught me that we can handle anything, if we have to." Maybe it was why Becca looked so sad all the time.

Actually, when Hannah knocked on their door for the first time, Bobby opened it but didn't look up at her.

"Mrs. Mooney, it must be hard to take care of such a big family. You are a brave woman."

"No! I'm not! I just do what I have to!"

Hannah reached over, lightly touching her arm. "I'm sorry. I'm here if you ever want to talk, and I promise, I'll listen."

Hannah Abbott and her mother Alice lived in the other second-floor apartment, right across from the Mooneys. They'd recently arrived in America from England. Hannah was round-shaped and beautiful, with a cheery disposition. Her mum Alice was an older version of her only daughter.

The Abbott women were unique to me because it was the first time in my history I could easily understand their English.

Alice was born in York, England, in 1904 and was the daughter of a chocolate maker, William Hewitt, who worked at the Rowntree's Chocolate Factory—one of the big three confectionery manufacturers in England. It was owned and operated by Quakers. Mr. Hewitt started his career by packing chocolates into boxes and worked his way up to making chocolate from scratch, using cocoa beans and other ingredients.

Hannah's mum, Alice, met her dad in 1920, when she started working at the same factory as a candy coater. They married a year later and had Hannah the following year. When she was eighteen years old, Hannah was also hired to work at Rowntree's. Then, the nightmare happened. On Wednesday, April 29, 1942, York suffered the worst air raid of World War II when a German Army aircrew dive-bombed York's neighborhood streets. Ninety-two people were left dead. William was among the hundred people injured, and he never recovered from his injuries. A week later, he died and their happy family no longer existed.

Years later, in 1951, Hannah and Alice decided to move to America to be close to her older brother, George—a chocolate maker with connections to the Fowler Chocolate Factory in Buffalo. He promised them both that his friend would help them get hired at the factory and also help to find them an apartment on the West Side, near his own family's residence on Fargo Avenue.

Alice sold her small home in York to begin their new life in Buffalo. Mother and daughter ended up as the Mooneys' neighbors on the same floor, and it didn't take long before all my tenants became curious about the sweet smell of chocolate in the building almost every day. It happened whenever Hannah and Alice came home from work. Most tenants could smell the scent of chocolate that clung to their exposed bodies and clothes. It wasn't long before I learned about how the taste of chocolate made people smile and want more.

One Saturday morning, when Bobby was sitting on my front stoop all by himself, Hannah started to walk past him on her way to buy groceries. "Hi, Bobby, remember me? I'm Miss Hannah and sometimes I talk to your ma in the hall."

He looked up and nodded.

"If you can wait a minute, I'll be right back with a surprise for you." When she came back, Hannah handed Bobby a small white paper bag.

"Thank you, Miss Hannah." He opened the bag and his eyes widened. No one had ever given him anything just for him. Immediately, he popped one of the small chocolate-coated caramels into his mouth and gave her a satisfied grin.

"I'll see you here again next Saturday morning at the same time," she said, smiling back to him. "Please don't tell anyone because the candy is only for you."

Bobby quickly jumped up and ran up the stairs and headed to his closet bedroom with his prized chocolates. He hid them underneath his blankets, near his pillow. His ma spotted him on his way out of the bedroom and told him to take out the garbage.

"Ma, when I'm done, will you help me with my spelling homework?"

"No. I can't. Can't you see I'm busy? You go out and play and be back by lunchtime."

His mother's response was always the same.

Bobby began collecting his older brothers' pencils and scraps of papers when they weren't home and placed them underneath his bedding. He would look for more writing supplies in the wastepaper baskets at school and in his neighbors' garbage cans. No one ever knew how much he liked to write—except me.

When Bobby was almost ten, Hannah became an important part of his life. About a month after they became friends, she asked Bobby's ma if she could take him to the library downtown the following Saturday afternoon after he had finished all his work. At first, Mrs. Mooney hesitated to say yes.

"Please, Becca, I'd like the company, and Bobby can get a library card and a book to read before he goes to bed at night. We won't be long."

"All right, but get him back here by supper."

Bobby didn't know what to say when Miss Hannah asked him to go to the library. He just looked up at her and smiled.

The Erie County Library was a lifesaver for him. The books he read took him into a different world, one where he could observe and learn the power of the written word. Bobby's favorite books became my favorites, too. He seemed to love history, like me. There was *Abraham Lincoln's World*, a children's history book, published in 1944, and *The Railroad to Freedom: A Story of the Civil War,* a fictionalized biography of Araminta Ros, later known as Harriet Tubman. It told of her life in slavery and her later work on the Underground Railroad and was first published in 1932.

Bobby wrote about how much he loved reading and writing, especially history, and the library became his safe place. The books talked to him, telling him their stories, and the characters within the books became his friends.

It was hard watching Bobby adjust to his unusual bedroom, but he did. After sleeping in the closet for several weeks, he noticed a creaking sound when he laid his head up against the right-hand side of the closet floor. His eyes widened when accidentally he discovered a secret hiding place. What Bobby didn't know was that this special place once contained a large boot box full of cash. It was where the Consiglios saved their money for their first home. Bobby quickly decided to use the secret hiding place for his writing so that no one would ever be able to find out and tease him or throw his writing away.

The next day, Bobby took his father's flashlight and a few extra batteries out of his old steel plant toolbox. He knew he'd be in trouble if his father found out, but he was prepared to lie if he had to protect his writing. Besides, I could tell by his smile how relaxed he was in his cramped quarters, mainly because this was the only time he didn't feel lonely. When Bobby wrote, he spoke the words out loud in a quiet voice that only I could hear—but he had to be careful so that his brothers wouldn't hear him.

I related to this lonely child because there were many times in my life when I was ignored and in desperate need of repairs. I worried about Bobby and realized that when he wrote in his tiny bedroom closet, he lost himself in his thoughts and didn't feel alone actually. It's the same way I feel when I listen and observe my tenants.

I wondered if it would be possible to communicate with him using telepathy.

Maybe I thought, just maybe, Bobby would want to be able to hear me. I needed a friend, too. Then, it happened. I saw him react. Suddenly, he looked around the entire inside of the closet, puzzled. He heard me, but he didn't know what to make of it.

I said, "Bobby, trust me. It's me, Fred, your imaginary friend. Talk to me, keep reading out loud, and I'll listen."

A few seconds later, he wrote and spoke an answer.

"I'll talk to you, Fred. You can be my friend."

Then, he quietly told me how his ma was always busy cooking, cleaning the house, washing clothes, mending, and caring for little Becky. "Then she has to wait on my pa and my brothers when they're home. Her eyes never looked into mine. She only yells at me and tells me to be quiet."

I understood that Bobby's closet was the quiet space he needed to sort out his feelings. Before he started to write, he would sit in the corner of the closet floor, legs crossed, scribbling. He drew circles, stars, and strange looking objects. His paper and pencils were magic. If he found a pen he could use, it was like gold. His words made his imagination come alive.

In 1954, when Bobby was twelve, his ma bought another cot for him to sleep on in the same bedroom with his brothers. Both brothers still laughed and joked with each other and continued to tease him. Only now his brothers were hardly ever home, and Bobby even had his own paper route because they really needed the money. Little Becky, now four, still clung to her ma. She was now sleeping in a part of the living room sectioned off with a clothesline covered with a blanket. She often cried out for her mother in the middle of the night.

Tragedy struck the Mooney family in 1955, the day after Bobby's thirteenth birthday. He was home and heard his ma scream and cry out his father's name. He ran into the kitchen and saw his father's lifeless body lying on the floor. He picked up Becky and hugged her closely and then reached for his ma. The three of them clung to each other. Then Bobby abruptly ran out into the hall and banged on Hannah and Alice's apartment door, crying for help. They came running into the apartment and made sure Bobby's mother got the help she needed. But it was too late; his father died while sitting at the table drinking nightly beer and fell over onto the kitchen floor. Now both his older brothers had to work full-time to help support the family. Becca's small widow's pension and Social Security were not enough to pay all their household expenses. Bobby had to work harder, delivering both morning and evening newspapers and keeping up with school. Since his father's death, Bobby felt closer to his ma because she paid attention to him, and he felt her love. Soon after Bobby's pa died, Bobby began drawing stick pictures of his father walking, until he disappeared on the paper. Then, he drew large falling tears, wet with real ones. I wept with him and felt his grief.

His ma remained depressed most of the time and hardly ever left the house except to buy groceries. His little sister Becky was becoming withdrawn. Bobby loved to read to her, but his ma would constantly stop him and tell him to go out and play or do some chores. Becky would cry when he left her.

"Ma doesn't feel good, Fred. I try to help her more, but it doesn't do any good. She cries a lot and keeps getting bad colds."

"I'm sorry, Bobby." I said. "It's all we have when we can't do anything else."

He took a deep breath and wrote my name and then three simple words: "I love you."

When Bobby said he loved me, I was speechless. No one ever told me they loved me. When I was first built, my Abigail loved my building because for her I represented freedom. Most of my tenants in the earlier years came from settlement and rooming houses. Living in a residential neighborhood for the first time in their lives was a significant accomplishment, and they loved living in one of my apartments.

But Bobby's love for me was different; he loved me like I was human.

The closet remained our secret pathway to friendship. His ma rarely went into his bedroom and never into the closet. Bobby hung an extra-large flashlight in his former makeshift bedroom so he could read anytime.

Becky was now six years old, and her older brothers were full-time construction workers. They both had girlfriends, and Bobby often had the bedroom to himself.

During the next few years, he wrote about Hannah and Alice and their experience working at Fowler's Chocolate Factory. He learned the history of Fowler's and wrote about that too. I learned that in 1901, Joseph A. Fowler traveled to Buffalo from Canada to participate in the Pan American Exposition, where he sold chocolate confections and sweets that he'd created. He and his brother Claude opened a small candy store selling a variety of chocolate confections on Jefferson Avenue in the city. It wasn't long before the Fowler's became chocolatiers, making their own candy from chocolate.

Hannah and Alice were hand-dipping nut clusters and barks at Fowler's. They would grab a handful of nuts and mix them quickly with chocolate. It was a job they enjoyed, and Bobby loved hearing about how chocolates were made.

Hannah made sure that Bobby had a chance to tour the factory and the chocolates. The day he took his tour was one of the best days of his life.

"Fred," he said, "doesn't my closet smell like chocolate? Look, they gave me another bag of chocolates to take home. I wish you could have one. I'll tell you how it feels in my mouth." Then, he pulled one out of his paper bag. "First, I smell it, then I put it in my mouth. I let it melt on my tongue before I chew it. It tastes so good."

I tried to imagine the flavor and enjoyed the fact that Bobby still smelled like chocolate.

He was only fifteen when his fifty-year-old mother died in 1957 from influenza. He knew in his heart that she loved him and depended on him to help her. Only there was no time to be hugged or kissed. His mother was never free to relax and enjoy any of her children, but there were rare times when he felt her love. Bobby told me he would love his ma forever.

Both of his brothers enlisted in the military—one chose the army, the other the navy. The day they left for military training, Bobby was interviewed for a full-time maintenance job at the Buffalo & Erie County Library. His brothers left without saying goodbye to him. It was a hard day for Bobby, and he went into the closet and cried. Little Becky went to a foster home and was adopted after a few months by a farm family in Eden, New York. He watched helplessly as his entire family disintegrated and began new lives without him.

Bobby asked me, "What will become of me, Fred? I have no home. No one wants me. I can't stay here. I'm going to leave before I get kicked out."

When he told me he was going to be homeless soon, I felt helpless. There was nothing I could do except hope for a miracle. The morning he was planning to leave, the thought of losing my friend was unbearable.

Then, something unbelievable happened. My Chocolate Ladies, Hannah and Alice, insisted that Bobby move in with them until he could get a job and apartment of his own. At first, Bobby said no, but they convinced him to stay, and our friendship continued.

No one but me ever knew how much Bobby loved to read and write. Not even Hannah. I always knew that his time in the closet would eventually have to end. I'd watched how a little boy became a man on the faded pages hidden in an old closet floor. For the last time, I saw Bobby pick up the boot box and look through his neat stack of notes and letters. There were tears in his eyes.

"Fred, I'm not leaving you. You'll be my friend for life. But I'm leaving my writing behind." It's when he carefully returned the box to its original hiding place.

It wasn't long before Bobby got the full-time job at the Buffalo & Erie County Library in downtown Buffalo, right across the street from the Hotel Lafayette.

Hannah and Alice still refused to take any money for his room and board. "You work and save for college. Mum and I love you. Earn a degree in history. We know how much an education means to you."

"I can't live here for free. You have to let me pay for rent." They refused, and each week Hannah and Alice received an envelope with a ten-dollar bill inside. Bobby didn't know it, but they never opened the envelopes and instead, kept them hidden in a dresser drawer. They both decided that the money would someday go toward his college degree.

Bobby's new job in the janitorial department at the library was perfect. There, he could work alone while surrounded by thousands of books, his favorite companions. He loved learning, and if he did end up teaching at a college or university, he could pass on his love of history. Bobby also cleaned the Thruway Tavern early each Saturday morning and saved all the extra money he earned.

In 1960, Bobby graduated from high school. He was proud but nervous about the possibility of being drafted into the Vietnam War. The day he registered for the draft was one filled with fear. The war was unpopular and death tolls were high on both sides. Bobby told me he didn't want to go to war and that if he had the courage, he would have been tempted to resist. He wanted to help people, not kill them. In the end, he felt it was his duty to go if drafted.

A year later, he applied to the State University College at Buffalo and was accepted as a part-time student. Bobby was so excited, he promised me he was going to become a history professor. I was so proud of him. Hannah and Alice promised to treat him to a special dinner at Santasiero's to celebrate.

"Thank you both for caring about me. I'll never forget how I was saved from becoming homeless."

"Bobby, you're special and we love you," Alice said, hugging him. "You're like a son to us," Hannah said in tears.

When they came home from their dinner, Bobby seemed to be standing taller. He was relaxed and happy. He gave Hannah and Alice a hug and told them how much he appreciated having a home and their support. Now he could work full-time and go to school part-time. I saw how a sad and lonely little boy became a confident young man on a mission.

Each night, Hannah and Alice would listen to the radio news programs. They also read newspapers, and both were concerned that Bobby was going to get drafted because of the growing conflict in Vietnam. Then, on September 10, 1963, President John F. Kennedy set up Executive Order 11119, which exempted married men 19–26 years old from the draft. Bobby realized that this order changed his draft status, putting him near the head of the line. Less than a year later, he was drafted.

Both Hannah and Alice cried and cried. He was going to be one of 230,991 draftees going to Vietnam. I was upset, too. Bobby grew up in my building—now he was going to go off to war. It would be a two-year commitment in the army, and after four months of training (half basic and half infantry), he would be assigned to the 4th Battalion, 17th Infantry Regiment, one of the first two divisions sent to defend the Republic of Vietnam.

When Bobby left for boot camp, it was traumatic for all of us. Would we ever see him again? I was afraid for his life and thought about what happened to my Benedict Farley who lost his life in World War II. During this time, Alice began suffering from severe pains in her hands and knees. They ached all the time, and it was getting harder and harder for her to go to work each day. Hannah tried to get her mum to stop working, but Alice was determined to work as long as possible.

Hannah and Alice sent care packages and letters to Bobby every week. My heart and prayers went with them. It was a difficult time for all of us.

We never knew exactly where he was, and his letters to Hannah and Alice were written in bunker tents whenever he could find the time. Some were short, and others were long and often stained. Sometimes I felt Bobby's presence and knew that he faced death every single day. Often, he would tell Hannah and Alice that he had lost another friend. He would explain that the enemy died as fast as our troops did. But all of his letters ended in the same way. "I hope I make it home. You're both my family, and my heart is with you."

I like to think that when Bobby said "both of you," he meant me too. In fact, I know he did.

In 1967, after a two-year hitch, Bobby Mooney came home safely from the war. Hannah and Alice hugged him tightly and wouldn't let go. I was happy too and couldn't wait to talk to him again. Bobby stayed in their apartment for a few days. Both women begged him to stay and live with them again. He refused but thanked them both. "You're both moms to me, but I'm a man now and need my own apartment near the University of Buffalo. I'm going to become a history professor."

Lucky for Bobby, his old second-floor apartment was empty at the time. He entered the apartment's closet the night before he moved out of Hannah's apartment and wrote his last letter to me.

Fred, I kept living while I heard men dying and crying for their mothers. I remembered what you said before I left. 'Bobby I'll be here for you as long as I'm still standing and feel your presence.' God saved me, Fred, and I don't know why. My friends' fates were sealed.

I'll never forget what it feels like to kill someone. After it happens, it numbs you and it gets easier when war rages around you. War is hell on Earth! I prayed over and over for it to end. I feel guilty because I lived through it. I'll always wonder why I was able to come back in one piece.

I'm going to teach history, Fred, and hope that my students leave my classes understanding how wars repeat themselves generation after generation. I'll challenge them to stay informed all their lives and to learn from the past. I'll plead with them to constantly question their leader's decisions, and if they lead others into war I pray it's a just war.

"Bobby, whenever you need me, I'll be there to listen. Goodbye, my friend, go live for both of us. Only please promise me you'll come back someday and share your life with me before evidence of my existence is gone."

"Fred, I won't let you down. It's a promise I vow to keep."

CHAPTER SEVENTEEN

. . . .

Freedom Fighter Refugees

Soon after Bobby Mooney left for boot camp in 1964, two good-looking men bounded up the narrow staircase to one of my fourth-floor apartments. I think they would have flown up the stairs if they could have. It was twenty-eight-year-old Zolton and his twenty-nine-year-old brother, Laszlo Popp, who were moving into their own apartment for the first time. They were Hungarian "freedom fighter" refugees when they first immigrated to Buffalo in 1957 from Communist Hungary.

When they first arrived in Buffalo, the brothers lived with their Uncle Tibor Popp, their deceased father's older brother and family, who were now proud American citizens speaking fluent English. Their uncle and other family members originally arrived in the United States under the Displaced Persons Act of 1948, which allowed certain people displaced by World War II to qualify for permanent residence. Tibor was one of many who were forced to work in German factories or farms, or those who survived concentration camps and were subsequently allowed to immigrate to America. After Zolton and Laszlo moved in, Uncle Popp came to visit his favorite nephews whenever he could, checking to make sure they were okay.

One afternoon, Hannah and Alice introduced themselves to the brothers when they all returned home from work at the same time. Soon afterward, they gave Zolton and Laszlo each a small bag of chocolates from Fowler's along with an invitation for authentic English food the following Sunday. I loved it when my Chocolate Ladies invited people to share food with them in their apartment, and it gave me a chance to learn more about their guests' history.

When Hannah and Alice served their English Sunday dinner to Zolton and Laszlo, I smelled their savory roast beef with hot white horseradish sauce, roasted potatoes, carrots, parsnips, and peas. It was served along with a Yorkshire pudding made from a batter of eggs, flour, and milk. For dessert, they served an English Trifle. It looked like some kind of cake in a large clear round bowl, with layers of custard, cream, strawberries, and blueberries—delicious. I wanted to be able to eat with them too.

Both brothers had two servings of Yorkshire pudding along with English tea. During dessert, they spoke about their American girlfriends who were sisters. "We are marrying our girlfriends as soon as we can afford to buy a two-family home. We want you both to meet them when you come to our Hungarian Sunday dinner in two weeks. Be prepared! We love spicy food. We are going to make what our mother and grandmother made for us and share some of our traditions with you."

"We can't wait!" Zolton said.

The brothers' told Hannah and Alice that their Uncle Tibor was their sponsor to the United States. He was responsible for finding both men employment that wouldn't replace another American worker. Thankfully, they were hired as laborers working on a variety of construction jobs. Zolton and Laszlo were excited when they were finally hired at the Mentholatum Company at 1360 Niagara Street, only a short walking distance from me.

The Mentholatum Company was an 80,000 square foot factory built in 1919. The brothers were lucky to be hired as two of seventy-five employees. The building had natural sunlight, was clean and spotless, and had modern equipment. The brothers couldn't stop talking about their new employer and its product, Mentholatum.

"It was made using crystals of menthol taken from hermetically sealed cans and compounding them in glass-lined tanks," Zolton said. "Our product is applied to the top of the skin for the cure of many inflammations, like sore throats, earaches, headaches, chapped hands, and more."

Hannah looked puzzled. "What does hermetically sealed mean?" she asked.

"We're really unsure," said Laszlo. "We use it now to impress you." They all laughed together and toasted each other with their water glasses.

I listened carefully and found out that the brothers worked together, boxing and packing products for distribution to every corner of the free world, filling orders in many different languages.

"We are proud, and we love our jobs," said Zolton. "This year, our company even donated nearly 200,000 jars of Mentholatum to help win the release of Cuban Invasion prisoners."

The brothers were from the city of Kalocsa, eighty-eight miles south of Budapest along the Danube River on the southern part of the Great Hungarian Plain.

Laszlo began their story. "We Hungarians spoke German before World War II, and German is still Hungary's second official language. The Russian language was mandatory in our schools and universities since the Socialist period. But in 1956, students began peaceful protests over the loss of our freedoms. Our Hungarian nation rose up against communist rule and oppression from the Soviet Union, and in a short time, we lost the battle to the Soviet tanks. We along with 200,000 of our fellow Hungarians fled to the West, escaping through the border into Austria."

"In 1957, we were lucky to be a part of the wave of immigrants who were welcomed to be resettled in America," Zolton said. "We were the youngest in the group of about 40,000 refugees who arrived in America with the help of the Hungarian Freedom Fund. We all were offered several forms of support, including financial assistance, employment, and educational scholarships."

"I will never forget the U.S. Navy's sealift and the C4 troop ship we came to America on," Zolton said. "We couldn't stop crying. We cried for our country, for our families, and for those we left behind, and for all our dead and injured friends."

Many of my tenants and their families also had to escape from the home country they loved. I admired all of them for their courage and determination to escape for freedom to America.

"We feel your pain," Alice said. "We know from our own personal experiences of war how difficult it must have been to come to America and start a new life. My Hannah's father was killed in the first bombing attack on of civilians in York, England, during World War II. We both know how it felt to be under attack."

"Thank you for sharing your loss with us," Laszlo said. "It's an honor to spend time with you both."

It was late in the evening when the brothers thanked their hosts for the wonderful food and invited them to come to their apartment two weeks later for an authentic Hungarian dinner.

Laszlo and Zolton then made a toast in Hungarian to Alice and Hannah. It was a night I'll always remember because they were all survivors of a war they never started.

It didn't take long to see my tenants' Sunday dinners became a bridge of friendship and understanding. All it seemed to take was an invitation from a stranger, and before you knew it, anyone who could come was welcomed. My immigrants and refugees appreciated being able to share their lives with others. I think they accepted each other's differences because they all knew they had something in common—the need and desire for freedom and opportunities in America to support themselves and their families.

It was good to see my Hannah and Alice make new friends because I knew Bobby Mooney was constantly in their thoughts. I was glad to see them relax a little. It was hard to see that Alice's health was failing and she was going to have to stop working soon. Her hands were often swollen with arthritis, and her knees were less reliable. Despite her illness, she was cheerful and never complained. It was hard to see her suffer in silence.

Zolton and Laszlo started cooking a week before their special Sunday dinner. Each night after work, they prepared a part of the meal, which consisted of chicken soup with Csiga noodles and Magyar (Hungarian bread), meatloaf, and cabbage stuffed with millet and rice, and chicken paprika made with garlic, tomatoes, and spiced chicken.

I learned all about Hungarian cooking when I saw them use their own noodle maker (*nokedli*) for the little dumplings. I was a silent guest, always imagining how delicious the food would taste.

My Chocolate Ladies arrived promptly at 1:00 p.m. and were greeted with kisses on both cheeks from Zolton, Laszlo, Lena, and Alicja Nowak, their Polish-American girlfriends. Then, their surprise guest stepped forward to meet Hannah and Alice. It was their Uncle Tibor Popp, who excitedly gave them each a bear hug.

The Popp brothers' apartment was spotless, and their guests complimented the young men on their housekeeping. "Our families were Catholic peasants, and their ancestors were Magyar Nomads. In Hungary, it's a custom to have a *"Tizta Zoba"*—a clean room— when we have special guests for dinner."

The table was already set, and off to the side, on a makeshift tray spread across a living room chair, were the desserts, which looked delicious. First came a drink of Tokaji, a Hungarian wine, which was served before dinner. Hannah and Alice also brought their hosts a large box of fine Fowler's chocolates.

Once everyone was seated and served, Hannah asked the brothers about the corner of the room filled with painted pictures and statues.

"This is our sacred corner," Zolton said. "These paintings are of our special saints, and the statues you see are from our Catholic pilgrimages. It's a tradition in Hungarian homes to honor our religion and our country's history."

Laszlo added, "Even our Protestant relatives and neighbors devoted a corner in their home to religious reformers, along with pictures of the leaders of the 1848 revolution."

Uncle Popp picked up the story from there. "It was during the revolution of 1848 that the Kingdom of Hungary fought for democratic reforms. Then, the revolution grew into a war for independence from the Austrian Empire. The beginning of that revolution is celebrated as a national holiday in Hungary every year on March 15th."

Uncle Tibor turned in his chair and pointed to the left-hand corner of the room. "See the painting on the wall. It's a picture of

Saint Stephan. He is special because he was the first King of Hungry and the founder of the Hungarian State. Because of that, we celebrate Saint Stephan's day every August 20th. We are a proud people and honor our holidays."

Uncle Tibor's face grew serious when he started to describe the unplanned uprising that lasted only twelve days before Hungary was crushed by the Soviet tanks and troops. "It started on October 23, 1956, when thousands of Hungarians were killed or wounded. A quarter of a million people left Hungary. Hungarians living in America feared the worst for their families and friends because they were unable to talk to them. It was horrible." When Uncle Tibor finished talking, the room became quiet, and I saw tears in his eyes. No one said a word, but their silence said it all, and watching their faces, made me want to cry too.

Alice spoke first. "It must have been a terrible time."

Zolton broke the silence when he got up from the table and said, "Our dinner isn't over yet. We made our special desserts for everyone. It's good to have dinner with our new friends."

Uncle Popp smiled and now looked relaxed. I wished I could tell the brothers how much I loved learning about their traditions, celebrations, and delicious smelling food. I can only imagine what it would be like to experience their lives firsthand. I am grateful to have Hungarian refugees living in my building.

Their dessert consisted of cream puffs made with a sponge cake batter. They resembled turbans worn by East Indians. Boy, did I want to be able to eat one.

Before the cream puffs were served, everyone had a bowl of cold peach soup, with a warm sugar syrup poured over it. The syrup was made with apricot brandy. Last, but not least, were the Kifli cookies—sugar cookies made with walnuts and cream cheese. I did try to taste them in my mind.

The entire dinner was a success, and they all promised to have Sunday dinner together again soon, and over the next several years, it became a tradition.

It wasn't long before Zolton and Laszlo succeeded in saving enough money to make a down payment on a two-family house in Black Rock near their relatives. They also saved enough money to help Lena and Alicja's family pay for their double wedding. The couples invited Hannah and Alice to their wedding celebration. Needless to say, my Chocolate Ladies were honored.

After the weddings, I heard Hannah and Alice reminiscing about how beautiful the brides were. "The couples couldn't have been happier," Alice said. "And who would have thought Uncle Popp would be such a good dancer."

"I think we were his favorite partners," Hannah said. Then, they both laughed remembering how much fun they had.

I was able to imagine what it might be like to dance and have fun, except I did feel like I was a part of the entire wedding. I was there in spirit and later saw all the pictures and heard my Chocolate Ladies relive the wedding with several other tenants.

It seems like whenever my tenants leave, I'm always saying it's a happy and sad time in my life. Although sometimes, it's heartbreaking. It's hard to accept change. It affects everyone and everything that exists. My building is constantly in transition. I have to consciously decide to view change as a companion rather than an uninvited guest. Change gives me strength once I accept its after effects. My tenants are all survivors, and I'm determined to be one too.

CHAPTER EIGHTEEN

. . . .

Unexpected Quaker Pacifist

I n 1971, anti–Vietnam War protests in the United States were well underway. It was during this time that a quiet, young twenty-three-year-old man, William Garrett, rented one of my fourth-floor apartments. He kept to himself and only left his apartment to buy food or go to an occasional movie. He didn't have a job or any friends that visited him.

It was hard for William to avoid Hannah and Alice, though, because they knocked on his door every day until he finally opened it and told them to please leave him alone. Quickly, they introduced themselves and gave him a bag of Fowler's chocolates. They usually made new tenants smile, but not William.

The following week, they invited William to dinner, but he refused. He said thank you to the Chocolate Ladies and immediately closed the door. The following day, Hannah and Alice knocked on his door again. Reluctantly, William agreed to eat with them the following Sunday.

During their first dinner together, Hannah and Alice discovered that William Garrett was a Quaker on his way to Canada. He was a pacifist and rejected any form of violence.

The women knew all about the Quakers because in York, England, their family had worked for the Roundtree Chocolate Factory owned by a Quaker family who supported working women and the women's suffrage movement, and Hannah and Alice knew the Quakers were against any act of violence.

Being a Quaker, William believed in the inner light and that everyone had an opportunity to connect with God directly in spiritual equality. He told both women that he had few friends, except for the pacifists and conscientious objectors who had already escaped to Canada. They promised to listen to William and to try to understand how he felt. I heard him heave a deep sigh before his flood of words began.

He was a descendant of Thomas Garrett, a Quaker born in 1789, who helped more than 2,700 slaves to escape from the South and was known as the "station master" of the final Underground Railroad station in Wilmington, Delaware. William was most proud of Thomas because nothing stopped him from helping slaves escape to freedom, not even the Fugitive Slave Act of 1850. His daughter, Alice Thomas Garrett, also worked with Harriet Tubman. In his heart, he knew that Thomas Garrett's legacy lived on through him.

"I'm a conscientious objector, and I didn't want to be forced to participate in the Vietnam War effort. Some of my friends are conscientious non-combatant civilians, who don't take a direct role in the war but offer their service as firefighters in Washington State, or work menial jobs in psychiatric hospitals."

I found that up to now, William had counseled conscientious objectors of all faiths and that a conscientious objector status could only be granted in the U.S. on strict religious grounds.

"Many young men were unable to qualify and fled to Canada, and I'm compelled to help them." William said.

"William, our Bobby Mooney was drafted into the Vietnam War for two years, and we are grateful that he came home safely." Hannah said. "He didn't want to go to war, and we didn't want him to go either," Alice said. "But he told us he didn't have it in him to avoid the draft."

"Mum, remember when he came home from the war, he was a changed man who witnessed firsthand the atrocities of war. Our Bobby believed that American soldiers' lives were taken in an unjust war. He vowed that when he becomes a history professor, he'll teach future generation of leaders to be honest and mindful of how to prevent rather than create wars."

William looked at Alice and Hannah and said, "I can empathize with Bobby's feelings." I saw him struggle with his words. "I care about all veterans and their families. Their lives are turned 'inside out,' and wars leave generations of heartaches behind that can never be mended. Our leaders make wars happen and combat troops pay the price. All I can do is to help those who try to escape the war.

I'm a descendant of generations of pacifists, and I'm living here in this building for a brief time before I head off to Canada to work with Momma Nancy Pocock, a Canadian Quaker and peace activist. When the Vietnam War began, she and her husband opened their home to the young men who crossed into Canada to avoid the draft. They also helped to provide shelter to people escaping from Vietnam. Her home was a safe place for refugees for decades. Nancy was born in the U.S. but moved to Toronto with her minister father when she was only ten years old, and in the 1950s, she became a Canadian Quaker and opened her home to all those fleeing the war."

"William, do you think you're making the right decision?" Hannah asked.

"Yes," he said. "I have no other choice. I want to work with Nancy to help support the U.S. conscientious objectors who didn't receive their conscientious objector status and are considered war resisters."

He told Hannah and Alice that his family had a long history of non-violence. "It's in my blood. My great-grandfather used to tell me a story when he was little about Cyrus Pingle, a Quaker botanist, who was drafted during the Civil War along with two other Vermont Quakers. Grandfather Cyrus would not bear arms, and his uncle tried to pay the $300 requested for his release, only he was jailed for several months and forced to go on marches carrying guns on his back. He was released only after President Abraham Lincoln personally intervened. So you see, how can I change who I am?"

"William, do you realize you may never be able to return to the U.S.?," Alice said.

"I'm sure I might be able to if draft resisters someday get amnesty—only time will tell. But one thing I know for sure is that if the dead could talk, there would probably be no more wars."

I'm sure that if William hadn't grown up in a Quaker family, he'd be different. He knew he was hated by the troops but prayed for their safety and honored their service to our country. He told the women that he constantly asked himself the same question, "If God could walk among us, would he be a Quaker? And his heart said yes!"

When dinner was over, Hannah and Alice gave him a large supply of chocolates to take with him when he left for his trip to Canada. They also invited him over for English tea, scones, and conversations at least two evenings a week.

They told William that they were his friends, and they cared about him.

A few weeks later, without notice, William Garrett was gone. He left the women an envelope with a request for them to pay the landlord the rest of his rent on his behalf, and another note thanking them for befriending him. He said he would never forget them. He believed that Hannah and Alice had the inner light and thanked them for their kindness.

Both women kept William in their thoughts and prayers each night hoping he would be able to return home to America someday.

As a Quaker pacifist, he had to be true to himself. I'll always wonder what became of William Garrett.

CHAPTER NINETEEN

· · · · · · · · · · · · · · · · · ·

America's Internal Migrants

I t wasn't too long after William left when two Puerto Rican families moved in across from each other into two empty apartments on the same floor. Fifty-year-old Rinaldo Torres and his forty-two-year-old wife Margarita moved into the first apartment with their twenty-year-old daughter Rocio and son-in-law Santo Flores. In the second apartment were Marco Rivera and his pregnant wife Milagros, who were the same ages as the young Flores couple. With them was Milagros's seventy-year-old widowed grandma Antonia, who recently moved to Buffalo from Puerto Rico.

The Torres' parents and Grandma Antonia spoke in a language I didn't understand, but, luckily, both young couples spoke English. While they were moving in, relatives and friends of both families helped them carry their mismatched furniture up the stairs.

I couldn't wait for Hannah and Alice to meet them and invite them to one of their special Sunday dinners.

It was a week before the Chocolate Ladies introduced themselves to the Torres and Rivera families. Of course, they'd noticed them the day they moved in but decided to go to the Buffalo Public Library first before meeting the families so they could learn about the Puerto Rican culture. They both brought the books home and read out loud to each other. This gave me an opportunity to learn that the language they spoke was Spanish and to also find out that Puerto Rico is a mountainous tropical island directly in the path of trade winds. It's composed of a large island and several small ones and has a rainforest, including both wet and dry climates.

I learned how the original people of Puerto Rico, at the time of the Spanish conquest, were the Taino Indians. They were peaceful, not like the warlike Caribs, who were cannibals, who came to Puerto Rico from the jungles of South America. Later, Spain brought African slaves to Puerto Rico to help the Spanish search for gold and to plant and harvest wheat.

My Puerto Rican families were different from all my other tenants because they were considered "internal migrants." That's because, in March 1917, President Woodrow Wilson signed the Jones-Shafroth Act, which gave Puerto Ricans U.S. citizenship. It also separated each branch of their government, giving individuals civil rights, and the U.S. Congress the power to veto laws passed by the Puerto Rican legislature. The U.S. controls the entire island including immigration, defense, mail services, and general affairs.

At first, the families were hesitant to accept their dinner invitation—they were never invited to dinner by non-Spanish speaking people. But Hannah and Alice were too friendly to resist.

After learning about their Puerto Rican history, I understood why they mistrusted strangers.

"We'll make you one of our special English dinners," Alice said. "It will be a little crowded in our apartment, but we love it."

Dinner the following Sunday night consisted of roast chicken, mashed potatoes, Brussels sprouts, and carrots. Their Puerto Rican guests loved the chicken and potatoes but were unsure of the other vegetables. What they did like was the banoffee pie made from bananas, cream, toffee, and condensed milk served with crumbled biscuits that were made with boiled butter and ice cream.

"We've been reading about your rich history and culture," Hannah said. "We didn't know your island was given up by Spain and later became a commonwealth of the U.S. Government in 1952."

"Our island always been taken away from us," Rinaldo said. "We live a double life. At home in Puerto Rico, we are accepted, and here in the U.S., we are considered foreigners, even though we are citizens."

"In our homes, we feel safe," Rocio said. "It's where we celebrate with our families and friends."

Grandma Antonia smiled and responded in Spanish after Margarita translated for her. "*Sí, Señoras,*" she said. "We take care of each other no matter what. We love to sing and dance when we celebrate holidays."

"We are hardly ever welcomed in this country," Marco said, lowering his head. "We are American citizens. The U.S. calls us internal migrants, but we face the same problems most immigrants do because Spanish is our first language and English is our second. This keeps us from getting better jobs in the United States unless we have a college degree and are fluent in English. We feel misunderstood and disrespected because of our differences, so we stick together with our own people."

"Please tell us more. Mum and I want to learn more about the Puerto Rican culture."

"We have two last names, one from our mother and one from our father. We are a mostly Catholic, multiethnic nation," continued Marco. "Tourism brings in the most income for our island. Santo, tell Hannah and Alice how we greet each other."

"With friendly handshakes and a nod of the head is how we do it. Men who are good friends hug each other."

"*Sí*, they do," Margarita added, "but with *Señor* or *Señora* by their title."

When Antonia interrupted in Spanish, they all smiled and let her talk. Milagros told her what they were talking about in Spanish. They all laughed.

"We don't consider interrupting each other to be rude," Rocio said. "We even stand close to each other when we talk. If someone steps back while we talk, we don't like it."

It was starting to get late, and everyone had to get up early for work the next morning. Before they left, Rinaldo and Margarita invited the ladies to come to an authentic Puerto Rican dinner on the first Sunday of the next month.

"We call our food *Cocina Criolla* (creole cooking)," Margarita said. "We'll make you some of our favorite dishes. We cook a mixture of Spanish, African, Taino, and American food."

It was good to see my Puerto Rican family letting down their guard with Hannah and Alice, and soon they were sharing even more information about their culture. I watched them become friends, and I wished I could sit at the table and talk with them too.

I appreciated all the dinners that Hannah and Alice had for my tenants and found out later that this was the last one. It was a unique opportunity to find out firsthand what their lives were like in their home country and in America. What I learned most from all the dinners was that food was the glue to friendships. Not all my tenants were invited to have dinner with the Chocolate Ladies, mainly because there was never enough time or space. But the food was how I learned about different cultures and how powerful sharing food is. It brings diverse cultures together in harmony.

In the meantime, Hannah and Alice continued reading about Puerto Rico. We learned that San Juan was the capital and largest city of Puerto Rico. It's a seaport on the north coast. In 1947, the U.S. gave Puerto Rico the right to elect its own government, and then on July 25, 1952, the island was transformed from an American territory to a Commonwealth.

During dinner with our new Puerto Rican families, we found out that they arrived in Buffalo in the 1950s as laborers returning to Puerto Rico before winter. By 1969, Mr. Torres and his son-in-law Santo were both hired by the Buffalo-based Pillsbury Flour Company. They were "baked cereal" makers who took oat flour and mixed it into a dough that was cooked and pushed through an extender and then came out Cheerios! Both men got their jobs because Santo's cousin, Carlos, worked there and vouched for their strong work ethic. They paid him weekly to let them ride to work in his old, beat-up Chevy.

Before the Torres and the Rivera families moved into their apartments, they had been crammed in a dilapidated house on Virginia Street. Then the young Riveras heard about my two available apartments from Father Anthony of Holy Cross Roman Catholic Church on Maryland Street. Then they were more than ready to move into clean, safe apartments of their own. Their jobs made it possible, and they felt blessed because they would still be neighbors. Now Grandma Antonia would be able to have her own bedroom instead of a sectioned off part of their living room.

Marco Rivera had a maintenance job cleaning offices and classrooms on the D'Youville College campus, and his wife Milagros was a nurse at Lafayette Hospital, a short walking distance away.

"We have strong family ties," Rinaldo said. "We stick together and want approval from our parents, grandparents, aunts, uncles, and relatives who live far away. My daughter Rocio works hard as a waitress at Deco's Restaurant and has applied for admission to Buffalo State Teachers College. She wants to become a high school teacher. Mama and I are proud of her and Santo."

I anxiously waited to see what their Puerto Rican dinner would be like and when Sunday arrived, I wanted to eat everything because it all looked good and smelled delicious.

There were a couple of main dishes. The first dish had fried beefsteak with sofrito, a mixture of onions, garlic, coriander, and peppers browned in olive oil and colored with achiote, bright yellow annatto seeds. Hannah and Alice couldn't wait to try each special dish. They kept repeating how grateful they were to enjoy their company and delicious food.

The second dish consisted of a roast leg of pork, flavored with adobo, a mixture of peppercorns, oregano, garlic, salt, olive oil, lime juice, or vinegar, rubbed into the meat before it was roasted.

"I made the asopao," said Rocio. "It's our traditional dish, and I hope you enjoy it. It's a gumbo that we make with chicken or shellfish. This one's with chicken. It's flavored with oregano, garlic, paprika, salt pork, pieces of cured ham, green peppers, chili peppers, onions, cilantro, olives, tomatoes, chorizos, and pimentos. Then, it's finished with green peas."

"This food is extraordinary," Hannah said, and Alice agreed.

I noticed how both Puerto Rican families talked with their hands and watched how they constantly interrupted each other's conversation. Hannah and Alice tried to keep up with them, only they needed more practice.

The flan (custard) dessert looked mouthwatering, and the sweet potato balls with coconut, cloves, and cinnamon topped off their scrumptious dinner.

"I'm happy," Antonia said, and everyone clapped, got up from their chairs, and hugged each other.

"Mum and I have been reading more about your culture. We honor all of you and thank you for this wonderful dinner."

It was a great success, and they couldn't stop talking about the smells, flavors, and beautiful colors of the Puerto Rican food. They were excited to be part of this unique celebration of friendship.

When Hannah and Alice entered their apartment after dinner, Alice had to sit down because she was in a lot of pain.

"Mom, shall I call the doctor?"

"No, Hannah, I'm okay, it must be my age, I'll be alright in a little bit."

When I heard her say she was in pain, I was worried too. She never complained, and it made me nervous, but the next day Alice felt better. In fact, she was excited when she found out about Hannah's new friend Chuck, a widower and an employee at Fowler's Chocolate factory. His wife passed away five years earlier. He was a chocolatier and reminded Hannah of her beloved father.

Alice did like Chuck and told Hannah how happy she was that she met someone who was kind and respectful.

"Hannah, maybe you'll marry him someday."

"Mum, we're only friends."

"I know, honey, but sometimes friendships can turn into a love affair like the one I had with your dad."

"Mum, I love you, and I miss my daddy."

In the spring of 1975, life in my building changed drastically when my dear Alice died in her sleep from heart failure. I was in shock and kept asking myself, "Why, why, did she have to die?"

If I could have had a "mum," she would have been like Alice. Life would never be the same without her. She was precious and made lifelong connections with my tenants. I'll forever be grateful to her for teaching me about generosity and kindness. I will miss her forever.

Alice's wish did come true when Hannah married her widower gentleman friend about a year later. She moved into his home in Black Rock and left me. I still miss her, her mum, and the wonderful smell of chocolate. Hannah was warm and friendly like her mum, and they both enriched my life and taught me the value of friendship.

Rinaldo and Margarita kept the same jobs and their daughter, Rocio, became a teacher at Lafayette High School. Her husband Marco was now a manager at Quaker Mills, and each family member owned their own car. Milagros became a nurse and later had a baby girl. Their grandma Antonia, now eighty, was still going strong. They all worked hard and supported each other, and their lives were a tribute to their strong family-focused culture.

· · · · · · · · · · · · · · · · · ·

CHAPTER TWENTY

Descendants of Enslaved
Peoples of Africa – Part I

I n the spring of 1992, I had two more apartments available on
the third floor. Soon two African American families moved in
only a week apart, and I found out that they were all friends like my
Puerto Rican families were. Over the years, I've noticed that when
my tenants first moved in most of them stayed within their own
culture for their friendships until they felt welcomed into a new
one. I constantly wished Hannah and Alice, my Chocolate Ladies,
were still here to welcome them. Then, I'd be able to continue to
have the benefit of their library research and discussions regarding
many of my tenants' culture and heritage.

I was excited to meet my first African American families and
wanted to be able to greet them personally. I was shocked to learn
that they were not immigrants, refugees, or internal migrants, but
were descendants of enslaved people of Africa.

The first family to move in consisted of forty-eight-year-old
Douglass Henson, his young wife, Kaisha, twenty-seven, and his
eighty-five-year-old mother, Granny Mattie Henson, who was the
mother of fifteen children.

She moved east to live with her youngest son Douglass and Kaisha three years earlier. Everyone called her Granny Mattie because she had thirty-one grandchildren and was a treasured member of their family. Her favorite pastime was to tell stories about their family's ancestors.

Granny Mattie's remaining children were now spread out throughout the country. They were teachers, nurses, ministers, doctors, and lawyers. All her family pictures covered an entire bedroom wall. On her dresser were pictures of all her children as babies and little wooden crosses for each of her five children lost in childbirth.

She was happy because living in my building allowed her to walk up and down Potomac Avenue when the weather was agreeable.

Douglass, her youngest, was only eighteen when he first left his family in South Carolina and moved to Chicago, Illinois, to live with his father's brother, Cordell, who worked for the Union Pacific Railroad. They were hiring, and Douglass hoped to get hired as a sleeping car porter by the Pullman Car Company.

Within a month, he was hired and worked long hours—400 hours a month, 20 hours at a time—helping passengers with their baggage, answering calls at all hours, making up sleeping berths at night, and turning them back into seating each morning. Douglass wasn't paid for morning hours because they were considered "Train Prep Training."

Douglass became a proud member of the Brotherhood of Sleeping Car Porters formed in 1925; it was the first labor organization led by African Americans. Their charter was granted by the American Federation of Labor (AFL).

In 1968, the Pullman Car Company went out of business, ending railroad operations, and Douglass lost his job. It's when he decided to move to Buffalo, New York, hoping to get a job at the Bethlehem Steel Plant in Lackawanna. He was lucky because he was hired within a month.

Douglass met his wife, Kaisha in the spring of 1982 when he was visiting his close friend Charlie at the Lafayette General Hospital located on the West Side of Buffalo. Charlie was in traction recovering from surgery on his broken elbow.

Kaisha was Charlie's nurse's aide, and Douglass would see her on the weekends when he visited his friend. She was a pleasant young woman who enjoyed her job. She was friendly and kind.

"Charlie, can you give me Kaisha's number. I'd like to ask her out on a date," said Douglass.

"Sure will. I know you like each other."

On the day Charlie was released from the hospital, Kaisha gave him her phone number for Douglass. He called her immediately and invited her out to dinner. They dated each other for a couple of months when Douglass received devastating news. On June 25, 1982, Bethlehem Steel announced it was closing its Lackawanna plant, laying off 8,000 remaining workers within six weeks. After fourteen years of working for the steel company, Douglass would be jobless.

It was a frightening time with so many people losing their good jobs all at once. Kaisha was sympathetic and supportive as Douglass adjusted to being unemployed for the first time in his life. After several months of unsuccessful searching, he applied for a Freight Handler Apprentice position for the Buffalo Southern Railroad. He was excited and relieved to be hired a few weeks later in early 1983. He felt like the luckiest man in the world to be hired back into the railroad industry. When Douglass finished his combination of on-the-job and classroom training, he was hired in the Gowanda, New York Yard, loading and unloading goods from trains.

Things settled down after he started working again, he and Kaisha started to plan for a future together. Then, the following spring, they were married.

In 1992, she received her acceptance letter from the D'Youville College Nursing Department. It was an answer to her prayers. It's when the couple moved into one of my apartments because it was within walking distance of the college. I'm so glad I was built in walking distance to schools and jobs—otherwise, maybe I wouldn't still exist.

When the Henson's settled into their apartment, they had a small, rickety, two-tiered wooden table in the living room. On it was a variety of objects including a collection of weathered-looking books and journals and yellowed scraps of paper containing words and stories. There were also many faded pictures of dark-skinned individuals who never seemed to smile. A tin box contained pieces of braided hair, brass buttons, small smooth stones taped on paper, scraps of brightly colored cloth, and a collection of various sized teeth. Another larger box contained a treasured slave and family journal.

Mattie told Kaisha and Douglass that her momma, Bella, constantly told her to be proud of who she was. "Mattie," my momma said, "tell your children and grandchildren we're descendants of survivors, and proud African Americans." It was exactly what Mattie did. She was proud, and there wasn't a day that she didn't talk about her heritage.

Each Sunday in their household was "Memory Sunday." First Mattie would get up early to help prepare dinner, and after dinner, when all the dishes were done, she'd open her two prized journals and repeat the stories her momma, grandma, and great-great-grandma told her, beginning in 1861. Mattie's words helped me visualize the trauma their past generations experienced.

I loved "Memory Sundays" and felt privileged to hear their ancestors' stories. Then, when it was time for Mattie to go to bed, she'd sit in her rocking chair thinking about all her children, grandchildren, and memories of her own childhood.

Each week she'd say, "Douglass, please write to your brothers, sisters, and grandchildren for me and ask them to write me about their lives. I want our family journal to be ready to share when I've gone to meet my Maker."

Douglass and Kaisha sat at the kitchen table at least once a week and wrote short letters dictated by Granny Mattie. She needed help because her spelling wasn't accurate and her hands were shaky. The letters contained life lessons, prayers, and inspiring thoughts.

In the middle of the living room table was a tiny vase holding artificial yellow daisies, small weed-like sticks, and a half-dozen small pieces of faded wheat. On the bottom shelf was Mattie's treasured collection of books.

The first was an original copy of Harriet Beecher Stowe's *Uncle Tom's Cabin*, an anti-slavery novel published in 1852. Harriet, an abolitionist, portrayed the reality of slavery and how it functioned as a lucrative business. The book was based on actual events from freed slave narratives and anti-slavery newspaper firsthand accounts. More than 10,000 copies were sold in the U.S. in just the first week.

The second book was written by abolitionist Frederick Douglass. He was a freed African American slave, social reformer, orator, statesman, and human rights advocate. He was born around 1818 in Tuckahoe, Maryland, and died in 1895. The book was an autobiography of his life titled *The Narrative of the Life of Fredrick Douglass, an American Slave.*

Douglass escaped from Talbot County, Maryland, in 1828 and fled to New York. He became a preacher and during the Civil War, assisted in the recruiting of colored men for the 54th and 55th Massachusetts regiments while advocating for the emancipation of slaves.

Mattie named her son Douglass in his honor, and their last name was passed down generations to honor Joshia Henson.

Frederick Douglass also had many white supporters, including William Lloyd Garrison and Isaac Knapp who co-founded the abolitionist newspaper, *The Liberator*, published weekly from January 1, 1831, until December 29, 1865. Douglass and William both helped thousands of slaves escape to freedom from the South on the Underground Railroad.

Beneath the Fredrick Douglass book was a large black and white faded picture of Harriet Tubman, wrapped in plastic. In 1849, Harriet, along with her two younger brothers, escaped from slavery in the Chesapeake Bay area of Maryland and fled to Philadelphia, Pennsylvania, following the North Star for guidance along the ninety-mile journey.

Once she made it to safety and freedom, it was Harriet's mission to rescue her family and others in slavery. In 1850, the Fugitive Slave Law was passed, requiring the return of escaped free slaves back to their southern plantations. Because of this act, in 1851, the Underground Railroad was rerouted to Canada.

Abolitionist John Brown advocated the use of violence to abolish slavery in 1858, and Harriet Tubman supported his efforts in the attack on slaveholders at Harper's Ferry, South Carolina. John Brown called her "General Tubman." Later, Harriet was on active duty for the Union Army during the Civil War. She was a cook, a nurse, and an armed scout and spy. She was the first woman to head an armed expedition during the war, leading the Union forces during the Combahee River Raid in South Carolina where more than 700 slaves were freed.

One evening, Mattie told Douglass and Kaisha that most slaves didn't know their actual birth date and couldn't ask their owners because if they did, they would be punished. "Your Granny Bella Henson made sure I knew all about the day I was born and our family history on your Momma's side. It's the only one she ever knew. Our men never had a chance to have a family for too long, and only a few families were able to be reunited. Your great-great-granddaddy died in the Civil War shortly after Grandma Harriet was born. He was a good daddy."

"Our slave journals are hard to read. But, there ain't nothing we can change. If we honor our history, then they didn't die in vain. Our people survived, with the help of Black and White abolitionists. Praise be to God."

"Granny Mattie," Kaisha said. "Whenever my brother, sisters, and I asked about slavery, my momma and daddy only told us that it was a terrible time. 'Someday when you're grown, we'll tell you more.' They told us over and over that there are good and bad people of all colors and to find the good ones because true friends are colorblind. Judge others by their actions, be fair-minded, and proud of your ancestors and yourself."

"Your momma and daddy were wise."

"I know, but I wish I knew my family's stories. Listening to you makes me feel proud to be an African American."

Mattie stopped talking for a minute to sip her tea and catch her breath before she continued reading her great-great-grandmother Pearly's slave journal.

I was treated better than field slaves, only I had to be ready to wait on them anytime during the day and night. When the master's wife was away from the plantation visiting her relatives, I had to sleep in the master's room. We were separated from field slaves. Our rich master gave us clothes, a set a year, and a pair of shoes. We got a suit of coarse wool cloth and two rough shirts. We saw slaves who were blacksmiths, brick makers, and woodcarvers, but couldn't talk to them.

I listened and learned that before the Civil War, field slaves had to sleep on beds made of wood with ropes stretched across with a straw tick top. The children slept under the bed on a trundle so that their mommas could reach down and help them if they got sick.

Not all slaves had beds. Many slept on dirt floors. They had no rights and couldn't learn to read or write, and if they got caught trying, bad things happened.

Slaves couldn't legally marry either but had large families, which the slaves' masters frequently tore apart by sale or removal. Slave children were presented to the master and became his property. Children who weren't sold worked carrying buckets and supplies to field hands.

Field slave children were raised on ash cakes and buttermilk. Ash cakes were small balls of dough made by using ashes raked out of a fireplace. The balls of dough were then put back on the hot coals and covered with ashes again. When they were cooked, they were taken out of the fireplace and the ashes were cleaned off and the balls were ready to be eaten. Slaves were often kept hungry, but they were usually allowed to keep chickens. Chickens helped them survive.

Mattie told them, "Chickens were killed and cleaned with the feathers left on. Then they were covered with clay and put in a hole in the ground and covered with hot coals. When the chicken was cooked, the clay was knocked off and the feathers were taken off too."

She also explained that slave children had no clothes and never knew what underwear were because they had nothing but a three-cornered rag. When a child survived and was older, their mother or relative would make them clothes out of anything they could find like discarded feed sacks.

"There were no clocks to go by, only the light of day," Mattie said. "When a slave was sick, the master called in a mammy who used roots and herbs to help heal them. If they were very sick, the overseer would call a doctor because they didn't want to lose their money-making property. Working in the rice fields took a horrible toll on slaves, and many died from terrible illnesses. That was when the master brought in more slaves to take their place."

Listening to her read the words in Pearly's journals over a period of weeks, I heard no outright bitterness, only prayers for freedom and sorrow for the loss of entire families. Pearly's only hope was that she'd survive long enough to escape to freedom using the constant light of the North Star. Thousands of people, including Pearly, escaped to freedom a step at a time. And the friends and relatives who never made it were forever etched onto Mattie's soul.

Their stories came alive on the pages of Pearly's slave journal— and they are stories I'll never forget. I heard how Harriet Tubman helped twenty-year-old and pregnant Pearly escape from the Brookgreen Plantation in South Carolina, along with four other slaves in January of 1861.

I was fifteen when I was kidnapped in South Africa and put on the Calhoun, a slave ship headed for the Charleston Port of Entry. I didn't have a name anymore. I was a number. I was sold to a slave plantation owner in Georgetown, South

Carolina. I had to take the last name of my master, the King of the Rice Plantations. His wife named me Pearly because I was a tall light-skinned African.

I was a house slave for my master's wife and she taught me how to read and write bible quotes when we were left alone. Us slaves weren't supposed to read and write. Then I learnt to sew and make her clothes. She called me a seamstress. Her friends wanted me to make them dresses to. I had to go to their plantations and they paid my slave master for my time.

I never gave my master and his wife a name. When I got pregnant at seventeen, my mistress knew it was her husband's child and everything changed. I heard my masters screaming and fighting with each other all the time, in the end the master won, and nothing changed except when I was alone with his wife. I got slapped hard and often. Sometimes my face was blooded. But she still had me make her dresses and I still prayed and hoped someday I would be free.

My masters three babies were all taken away from me when they were born. I couldn't even hug them. My baby boy and two girls were taken care of by a field slave and right before they were one year old they were sold. At twenty I was expecting again.

I still worked for other plantation owners wife's. During one of my visits to Laurel Hill Plantation, by the Waccamaw River, I met a slave servant named Leroy who looked into my eyes and I knew we would find a way to talk.

After three more visits, we were able to sneak notes to each other. He could read and write but kept it to himself. He was twenty-three when he was given to his master by the master's father when he died. He was a mean man and beat

Leroy. Leroy learned to cow tow to his master but was strong as steel inside.

I was waitin for the plantations mistress to come out and take me to her dressing room. When she came to take me to the dressing room, the masters child cried and the mistress left my side to get her. Leroy walked by me and gave me a note with a picture of a star and arrow and the word free.

Each Sunday as Mattie read from Pearly's journal, I felt her pain and couldn't believe what she and her people endured. It was heart-wrenching. But on one particular Sunday, I longed to jump inside her journal and surround Pearly with love.

My Leroy was brave. We both could have been beaten to death. My dress pocket felt like it was on fire. I read Leroy's note on Sunday when the family went to church. I said yes! When? Where? How? I prayed to God for the month to go by fast. I got to travel to Leroy's plantation on the first Wednesday of the next month.

I chewed up his monthly notes the first year we met. I was scared we would get caught reading and writing and get whipped or have our fingers and toes cut off. We both were lucky because our slave holders secretly taught us how to read and write. They didn't know they helped us escape to freedom instead.

I ran away to the North following the North star with Leroy and eight other slaves when I was six months pregnant with my master's child number four. This baby was goin to be born free thanks to Leroy and Harriet Tubman. In 1860, we all left during the Christmas holiday when our plantation masters had dinner with the family and friends. My Leroy was with Harriet Tubman's two younger brothers, Ben and Henry, who ran away north to Pennsylvania with her. They set the plan in motion and Harriet met us in the woods and took us to the Underground Railroad and safe houses on the way.

Pearly's daughter, Harriet, was born in April, shortly after the Civil War started, and was named after the abolitionist, Harriett Tubman. Pearly and Leroy were married as soon as they were free, and he became a real daddy to her child. Leroy Josiah Henson was the name he gave himself on their marriage certificate. Josiah Henson was the man who wrote *The Life of Josiah Henson, Formerly a Slave, Now an Inhabitant of Canada*, narrated by Henson himself in 1849. It was published three years prior to Harriet Beecher Stowe's novel, *Uncle Tom's Cabin*. It is believed that her character "Uncle Tom" was based on Josiah's life as a slave. Pearly and Leroy learned all of this from stories they were told as they traveled north.

On the day of their marriage, Leroy told Pearly, "I'm a free man, and Josiah's my hero. You are gonna now be Mrs. Leroy Josiah Henson."

On another Sunday, I listened as Mattie read a few more lines describing how Pearly felt when she was on the slave ship.

We were separated and stacked up like a forest of stacks of wood. Can't say one more word about it. Can't do it. No need for you to know how I was feeling. Many people died, and us who lived were held on Sullivans Island in South Carolina before we were sold in a slave market. They treated us like animals.

Harriet Tubman helped us escape to the North. She took her seventy-seven-year-old mother and father before the Civil War. Harriet went back and into the slave country nineteen times by 1860. We call her Moses of her People. She helped Quaker Abolitionist Levi Coffin and his wife Cathrine who helped over 2,000 slaves escape to freedom.

On January 1, 1863, The Emancipation Proclamation freed slaves in states still in rebellion. It freed blacks to join into the Army of the United States. Frederick Douglass recruited my Leroy into the 54th Massachusetts Infantry put together by the Bureau of Colored Troops in the spring of 1863.

Then, suddenly, Mattie put her journal down, lowered her eyes, and cried.

"Momma, what's wrong? Why are you crying?"

"Douglass, there are tear stains on the bottom of this page."

"How do you know they're tears?"

"I know, Douglass, I know because of what Pearly says next."

My Leroy died. He took part in the infantry assault on Fort Wagner. It was filled with Confederates guarding the entrance to Charleston Harbor. The 54th Infantry Division was made up of mostly free northern black men. They suffered terrible deaths. It was the day my baby Harriet lost her daddy.

Mattie stopped again. "After that, your Granny Pearly worked as a seamstress and made enough money to support little Harriet and helped Harriet Tubman and the abolitionists as much as she could."

When Mattie was tired of reading, she'd put Pearly's journal down on her lap. Douglass would pick it up and put it in its proper place while Kaisha gently kissed her goodnight. I wanted to kiss Mattie goodnight, too.

Words can't express how deeply I feel about Granny Mattie and her family. Their ancestors passed on generations of a proud African bloodline through Pearly's slave and family journals. Granny

Mattie is a hero and guardian of the truth. Her journals make past generations come alive on their fragile pages. They contain the courage and strength of her African ancestors, and their struggle for freedom in America.

· ·

CHAPTER TWENTY-ONE

Descendants of Enslaved
Peoples of Africa – Part II

F orty-five-year-old William (Willie) Still Freeman and his wife
Sojo Truth Burris lived in the same East Side Buffalo apartment
house on Peach Street where the Browns lived, and it's where their
families became best friends.

When the Freemans moved into their apartment, Willie was
already a successful barber. Living here allowed him and Sojo to
continue to save for a home and barbershop of their own on the West
Side. Sojo was a social worker for Catholic Charities and worked with
immigrant populations in the neighborhood. They both believed
their hard work and ability to save money weekly would help them
buy a home of their own and buy a small barbershop that would
secure their future.

After the Freemans were settled in, I noticed that their second
bedroom was turned into a cheerful sitting room with a carpet,
three worn comfortable-looking chairs, and a small table with a
delicate vase containing a fresh red rose.

One side of the small room wall held a collection of framed
photographs of an infant child in different stages of development.
Then, I saw a large picture of a smiling little girl about five or six

years of age holding a brown teddy bear. Beneath the pictures was the same rocking chair with the same teddy bear I saw in the picture.

The table also held another framed photograph collection of their youngest daughter Trudy when she was a little girl. She was now a Buffalo Police Officer on the West Side of Buffalo in District 10's Niagara Street Station. Sojo and Willie were proud of Trudy and happy when she stopped over weekly to have a cup of coffee with them in their special sitting room. When she left the apartment, she always took the time to check in on Mrs. Mandy Mixon, who lived alone on the first floor. It was something she did when she worked the night shift. Trudy was the only person Mrs. Mixon would talk to growing up. They had a special bond, and she worried about her being the only person living on the first floor.

I was sad when I learned that the Freemans' first child, Mesha, died when she was only eight years old from a nasty cold, chills, and a high fever. It happened at bedtime when all of a sudden, Mesha had a hard time breathing. They rushed her to the hospital immediately, taking Trudy with them because there was no one to watch her. Mesha died that night in a coma. It was an overwhelming shock. Trudy had a hard time understanding what happened to her older sister. All she did was cry when she thought about her. There was nothing the Freemans could do to make their grief disappear or spare Trudy from the truth. I was heartbroken too when I found out about how their little Mesha died.

The night it happened, Willie and Sojo wished they could wake up from the nightmare and find Mesha sound asleep in her bed. Little Trudy constantly woke up in the middle of the night crying in the same bedroom she had shared with her sister. She would go screaming into her parents' bedroom. They comforted her the best they could while their hearts were breaking. Eventually, Mesha's bed was given to a family who couldn't afford to buy one for their child.

Over the next several years, the Freemans promised that when Trudy was grown up and moved out on her own, they would use the extra bedroom as a cheerful sitting room in remembrance of their first child, Mesha. Now that Trudy was no longer living with them, they were able to create their special room. It was a peaceful place for all of them to sit and talk when Trudy visited.

It was a comforting room filled with childhood memories of both Mesha and Trudy; she was an independent and curious child, and when Trudy came to visit, the Freemans invited Douglass and Kaisha to join them for coffee and dessert in the sitting room. They were close friends since Trudy was a child and enjoyed spending time together whenever possible.

One Sunday when they were all together, I found out just how inquisitive Trudy was as a child. Willie started the conversation first. "I remember when you first asked your Momma why did Mesha die?"

"I remember," Trudy said. "Momma told me she had no answer. Then you said, 'All we can do is pray for her, cry for her, miss her, and love her memory.' Daddy, you were right, there are no answers. Her short life is a blessing to our family."

"Trudy," Sojo said. "I remember that after we tried to answer your question, you said 'Momma and Daddy, I'll pray for her and us too.'"

I listened as often as possible to their stories of Trudy's childhood and heard more of the questions she asked as she grew older.

"Daddy, why are we born Black?"

"Because God makes people in all different colors."

"We have to make the best of our lives and be proud of our heritage. Remember everyone is special, even ants and plants," Sojo said, smiling.

"Why couldn't I go to my best friend Suzy's birthday party?"

"Why didn't I get invited?" Trudy said.

"I don't know, Trudy. What did Suzy say?"

"She didn't say anything except that her mom told her no. Suzy was mad at her mom."

"I'm sorry, Trudy. But when you grow up, you can make sure that your children can invite whoever they want to. Appreciate everyone, Trudy. Be a role model for others."

In high school, Trudy learned how to handle the students who tried to pick on her. Mainly, she ignored them. Instead, she concentrated on studying hard and earning good grades. She smiled often and slowly made friends with other kids more vulnerable than she was. One day her social studies class went on a field trip to a Buffalo Police Station in her neighborhood. The police officer talked about his job and encouraged the kids in the class to consider police work as a profession after they graduated from high school or college. Then, Trudy asked an important question.

"Are there good and bad police officers?"

The police captain thought for a moment before he answered.

"Well, I believe most people in this profession joined the force to serve the community at large. Most police officers are honest and treat people with respect following the law. They see the best and worst in people and make life-saving decisions. We want an honest and diligent officer on the force. On rare occasions, there are cops that need to be reminded of what it means to be a good role model to our citizens. If they break the law, they must be accountable. Overall, cops are dedicated individuals. They have families too and have to try to leave their experiences on the job when their shift is over. It's tough to balance their job and their personal lives, but it's a rewarding job."

When Trudy got home from her field trip that day, she told Sojo and Willie that she was going to become a police officer.

"I want to make a difference. You both taught me to be proud of my heritage and to be respectful of others. I want to be a good role model, respectful of everyone."

After graduation from high school, she was hired as a receptionist in a doctor's office. In her spare time, she practiced sample Civil Service Police Officer exams months before the exam was given for the Buffalo Police Department. Trudy scored high on the list. It took several months before she was hired as a police officer. She was twenty-three years old when her training was completed. After graduation from the academy, the Browns and Freemans took Trudy out to dinner to celebrate her accomplishment.

The Freemans were proud of their daughter, and when she came for her weekly visit, the Browns hoped they'd be able to see her, too. They were close to Trudy, and she considered them her auntie and uncle.

Actually, Trudy was friendly to everyone, especially Mrs. Mixon, the World War II widow who lived alone in the first-floor apartment.

On another Sunday morning when Trudy and the Browns were having coffee together, Willie was extremely talkative. It's when I found out that the Freemans married quickly in 1965, right after they both graduated from East High School because Sojo became pregnant. They were married in early June, just after Willie registered for the draft on his eighteenth birthday, and Mesha was born in the fall. The couple had no choice but to stay with his widowed father in his small cottage on Grape Street. The following year, Trudy was born.

In 1968, without telling anyone, Willie enlisted in the Marines for a three-year hitch. When Sojo found out, she picked up her little girls, Mesha and Trudy, held them tightly, and cried, panic-stricken.

"I remember our entire conversation," Sojo said. "I was shocked and scared. I couldn't believe you made your decision to go join the Marines without talking to me first."

"I kept asking you why, Willie? Why did you join the Marines to fight in Vietnam? I remember saying that we have two kids and what if you get killed or injured? Then, I started crying."

"I remember that too, Sojo. I did it for us and for our family because I couldn't get a good job. We needed a steady paycheck and benefits for you and the girls. I loved you and our daughters to heaven and back and promised I would come home safely. I remember telling you that my daddy would help you while I'm away, but you couldn't stop crying."

"I know, Willie. I understand it now, but at the time, I was so scared. When my tears finally stopped, I knew I had to be strong for our children and for you too. It was a courageous thing you were doing for our country."

Willie became part of a Marine Battalion stationed to the south of Da Nang. Their losses were high, and Willie was one of the lucky ones who returned home safely from the war. But he carried internal scars and silent anguish for the troops who would never return to their families. Willie's Bronze Star for bravery remained hidden in his bottom dresser drawer until he was alone in the apartment. For him, it was a constant reminder of a senseless war. He never told his family about how he felt, but more than a few times I saw him open that drawer and take out his Bronze Star and a large envelope filled with pictures of his deceased and wounded buddies. He'd get on his knees and sob with his head buried in his hands. Watching him was sad. I wished I could comfort him or hold him tightly.

Willie was bitter because when the Vietnam veterans came home from war, they weren't welcomed like other veterans from past wars. The soldiers had fought as their government leaders had asked them to. They did their duty to their country and were shocked by people's anger and disrespect when they came home from the war. To become the target of their country's anger was traumatic. Willie believed it was important to help veterans and volunteered as often as possible at the Buffalo Veteran's Administration Medical Center.

"Willie, you never shared that story with us before," Douglass said.

"It is something I never talk about but right now it feels good to share it with all of you."

"It's good to talk about our pain sometimes," Sojo said.

Willie and Sojo's family overcame many hardships, especially the loss of their first child. When they first moved into their apartment, it was a dream come true. Their daily lives were a tribute to the Freemans' strength of character because family was everything to them. They honored the past and lived for today. It's what I've decided to do too.

I saw Willie and Douglass sitting on my front stoop on a Saturday morning, coffee cups in hand. I listened when Willie started telling Douglass about his childhood. "When I was a young child, my father began to tell me stories about my great grandfather. Douglass would come into the bedroom each Sunday morning with a cup of coffee in one hand and a peeled orange in another. I'd sit up in my bed, bunching my pillow behind me, eating my orange."

"I bet you can still taste that orange."

Willie nodded and continued talking. "When I was a little older, my father explained that in our family, all firstborn sons were named after William Still who was born a free Black African American in Philadelphia, Pennsylvania, before the Civil War. He was an abolitionist who often financed and helped his friend Harriet Tubman on her trips south to rescue slaves. He was an important conductor of the Northern Underground Railroad, finding safe routes for slaves to reach freedom.

"We found out more about him when Trudy was in high school. It happened when her social studies class had to research a historic figure, and she chose William Still. During her research, she found out that after the war, Still wrote and published *The Underground Railroad* with his own detailed records and stories of the slaves who escaped from the south, along with letters from abolitionist supporters and friends like Thomas Garrett and Frances Harper. Trudy even found William's 1902 Obituary in the *New York Times* where he was called the 'Father of the Underground Railroad.'"

"Wow, Willie," Douglass said. "I'm surprised. Why haven't I learned about him?"

"I know. There are many important African Americans we've never heard about. But that's another conversation."

"So," Douglass continued, "When did your naming tradition begin?"

"Well, my great grandfather was the first to do it in my family. His parents were slaves who won their freedom at the end of the Civil War. That was when they took the last name Freeman for themselves. They made their way to Allegany County in Pennsylvania because there was work to be had in the coal mines. They knew all about the Underground Railroad and the stories of the daring people who helped make it work. When my great grandfather's first son was born, they named him William Still Freeman in honor of the important man they admired. He worked so hard to help our people escape to freedom.

"When William was old enough, he went to work in the mines with my great grandfather. Then, when he was twenty-five, he left the mines to work as a porter for the Pennsylvania Railroad. That's when William married and started a family. After two daughters, their first son, my grandpa, was born in 1902. My great grandparents decided to continue the legacy, and my grandfather was named William Still Freeman, Jr. It was in the same year of 1902 that William Still died in Philadelphia at the age of eighty.

"My grandpa became a railroad man, too, and in 1920, he married my grandmother, Alfreda, the love of his life. Shortly after that, he heard about a good opportunity with the Lehigh Valley Railroad, and they moved to Buffalo to take it."

"I wondered how your family ended up in Buffalo." Douglass said.

"It turned out to be a pretty good move for all of us."

Just then, Sojo came out the front door and called to the men. "Good morning, Douglass. Sorry, but I've gotta take Willie away for now. We need to go get our shopping done."

"That's okay, Sojo. I understand. We're out of coffee anyway."

"Okay, honey, I'll be right there." Willie said.

"Douglass, we'll finish our conversation another time."

It was a few weeks before Willie could join Douglass again for coffee out on the stoop. It was another sunny Saturday morning, and the traffic moved slowly along Niagara Street. After they talked about current events and baseball scores, Douglass turned the conversation back to Willie's family story.

"What year did you say your grandparents moved to Buffalo? Was it in 1920?"

"That's right, Douglass. They lived on the East side, and Grandpa worked as a Dining Car Waiter on the Maple Leaf Express."

"My father was born in 1922, and there was no doubt about what his name would be. He was named William Stills Freeman the third." Willie said.

"Things were going well for my family for a long time until the Depression hit in 1929. My Grandpa lost his job because of his low seniority, and he had no hope of going back to work soon. He shined shoes, helped a barber clean his shop, swept streets, and emptied garbage cans to make money. My Grandma helped, too, by cleaning houses for wealthy doctors.

"I learned that during their hard times, what really saved them from endless soup lines and long-term assistance was Grandpa's saved 'house money.' It took him nine years to save $800 toward the home they hoped to buy. But even with that, by the end of 1934, they had to apply for public assistance." By then William's father was twelve years old, running errands and doing any odd jobs after school to help the family out.

Things were desperate until President Franklin D. Roosevelt's Public Works Administration funds arrived in Buffalo. Then, his Grandpa was hired to work on a massive sewer construction project in Buffalo from March 1936 until June 1939. At the time, it was considered one of the country's largest projects.

His luck continued when his former supervisor on the Lehigh Railroad helped him get rehired as a waiter on Lehigh Valley's flagship train, the Black Diamond streamliner, which traveled between New York City and Buffalo. They called it the "Honeymoon

Express" because newlyweds took the train to Niagara Falls. After that, Grandpa stayed with the railroad until he retired.

"I thought working on the trains would be an interesting job," Douglass said.

"Yeah, me too. My Grandpa said it was hard work, but he loved meeting new people and he had the right personality for that job."

"How about your dad?" Douglass asked. "Did he ever want to be on the railroad, too?"

"I don't think so. When he finished school, he worked with a neighbor who was a carpenter. He was always pretty good with his hands. He was twenty when he and my mother married, and then he went right into the army because World War II had begun. He fought in Europe from 1942 to 1944. When he came home from the war, he and my mom lived with my grandparents until my sister, Carrie was born. Then, dad got hired at the GM engine plant on River Road, and at last, they could afford to get an apartment of their own. And then, I came along in 1947—William Still Freeman, the fourth!"

"Willie," Douglass grinned, "it's an impressive title! And a unique one. How lucky it was that your dad knew his family history and shared it with you. There aren't many of us who can trace our roots back generations. I know I'm fortunate to have Granny Mattie and our family journals."

Listening to their conversations gave me an awareness that everyone's stories are valuable. It made me wonder how Sojo got the name Sojourner Truth. I was hoping someone would ask her. It finally happened one Sunday when the Browns joined the Freemans for coffee. Kaisha commented on Sojo's unusual name.

"My Momma told me many times growing up that I'm named after the Civil Rights and Women's Rights activist, Sojourner Truth, just like my grandma was."

Sojourner was an African American abolitionist, born a slave in Swartekill, New York, around 1797. She was one of twelve children, and after the death of their slave owner, they were all separated, and nine-year-old Sojourner was sold at an auction, along with a flock of sheep, for $100. She was sold two more times before escaping with her baby daughter to freedom in 1826.

"I still have a copy of her book of memories, which she dictated to her friend because she could not read or write. In her dedication, Sojourner also included William Lloyd Garrison, the abolitionist, publisher, journalist, and activist."

"Is that why you became a social worker?" Kaisha asked.

"My namesake inspired me. It's an honor to be named after an African American abolitionist, and it made me want to make a difference in children's lives and make them realize how special they are. Many of the immigrant families I work with have gone through terrible hardships, wars, and separation from their families. It's rewarding to help them feel safe and to thrive in America."

"My ancestors had people who helped them too," Sojo said. "My great grandfather, Samuel, had a close friend named John Henry Hill. He was a twenty-five-year-old slave carpenter from Richmond Hill whose wife and children were free in Petersburg, Virginia. In 1853, he was able to escape when the William Still Vigilance Committee provided $125 for him to have a private room on the steamship named the *City of Richmond*, headed for Canada."

"My grandpa was on that same steamship, which was scheduled to stop in Philadelphia en route to Canada. He was twenty years old and alone when his mother, brothers, and sisters were all sold separately and his father died in the rice fields." Sojo said.

"Because of the Fugitive Slave Law of 1850, John Henry changed his plans of going to Virginia and headed to Canada instead. His wife and children planned to join him there when he was settled and could provide for them."

"John Henry befriended my grandfather and offered him a chance to learn how to be a carpenter and bricklayer promising that they both would be free."

"Samuel happily accepted, and they settled in Hamilton, Ontario, where my grandpa became a skilled tradesman like his friend and mentor John Henry."

"Please continue and tell us more," Kashia said. "It's good to hear more about our history in America."

"Well with John Henry's permission, Grandpa Samuel changed his name to J.H. Hill in honor of his best friend. Then, he married Alicia, a freed slave from South Carolina. When the Civil War ended, the couple moved back to the United States, to Gettysburg, Pennsylvania, to be closer to his wife's relatives. And that was when they named their firstborn daughter Sojourner Truth Hill, Sojo for short. It was surprising to find out another reason for former freed slaves to pick new names when they were finally free because they no longer had their original names. They lost them on the slave ships. It wasn't unusual to take the name of former slaves and abolitionists who were brave and heroic. It was a way to honor and remember them."

It was shocking to hear what it was like to be enslaved. I wondered how a human being was capable of inhumanity to another human being. But when I look back in time and think of wars and discrimination, there are no answers only questions. I focus on all the good qualities my tenants and families had, and I have hope for the future. Without it, I believe our fate is questionable.

One evening, Sojo told Mattie that her maternal grandparents' family journals containing all their oral histories were destroyed when their house was burned beyond recognition in a horrible fire in 1890. Sojo's grandma's little brother, Daniel, died because they couldn't reach his bedroom in time. It took many years for their family to come to terms with his tragic death. They honored his life by adopting a young orphan boy three years later. It gave the family peace to know that their adopted child would grow up in a loving home like little Daniel would have, if he'd survived the fire.

In 1906, Granny Sojourner moved from Pennsylvania to Buffalo with her husband, Emmett, and their two sons. J.H. and Alicia, her parents both refused to move. It was difficult for my Granny to leave her parents behind.

"Sojo, honey," Mattie said. "I understand their heartache. I've had to leave people behind too. You never get over it."

Sojo continued. "Grandpa Emmett was a bricklayer/handyman, who saved enough money to make a down payment on a small apartment building on the East Side of Buffalo. Their family of four lived in the small first-floor apartment. When my mother, Grace, was born a few years later, their family moved to the larger upstairs apartment."

Through Sojo's stories, I learned how special Africa is and how her grandpa told his children to be proud of their roots. Her momma made sure she honored her heritage and cooked traditional African foods for her children. It included okra, black-eyed peas, and kidney and lima beans, including watermelon, coconut water, hibiscus, beet juice, and blueberries that originally came from slave ships on transatlantic voyages.

Sojo's momma shared all her Grandpa's oral stories, just like he would have if he were still alive. Grandma Mattie told an amazing story about America's first cowboys, and she always smiled when she told this story.

"I found out that when the Civil War was over, that the 'African Cowboys' were actually listed in Slave Plantation Records." Grandma Mattie said.

"Sojo, it's a secret most people in America don't know about."

I learned that the Fula people from Senegambia became slaves and their longhorn cattle were imported to South Carolina in 1731. When the Civil War was over, their cattle were transported to Texas and were renamed Texas Longhorn Cattle with no mention of where they originally came from.

"There are so many stories waiting to be told," Mattie said.

"I know Grandma Mattie, I have another one to tell."

Sojo continued to talk. I was shocked to find out that 882 ships arrived on Sullivan's Island, South Carolina, with an estimated 260,000 Africans. They too lost their identity and homeland on their way to America. I can't imagine what it must have felt like. My heart hurts for everyone who was enslaved.

"Most of the slave ships our descendants traveled to America on came through Charleston Harbor to Sullivan Island in South Carolina," Willie said.

"I know," said Mattie. "It's where I want to be buried."

"Does anyone know how many African slaves were on the 882 ships that arrived on Sullivan's Island?" Kashia asked.

No one could answer, except for Willie who remained silent, but then spoke up.

"There were an estimated 260,000 Africans who lost their identity and homeland on their way to America. We are all a part of the 80 percent of slaves who arrived in South Carolina."

I saw them all stop talking when Granny Mattie sighed and looked like she was about ready to cry. The statement was a sobering moment of truth, and they were united together in their hearts and souls.

I wanted to let them know that their legacy would be sealed on the pages of this humble novel.

The Browns and Freemans were my last official tenants. Granny Mattie lived ten more years before she was laid to rest on old Sullivan's Island, South Carolina, where it all began. She would always tell her son and daughter-in-law, "I'm saving my pennies and dollars too so you can take me back and bury me where my ancestors landed. Bury me facing eastward, facing Africa."

"Momma," Douglass said. "We'll honor your wishes."

I will never forget Granny Mattie. She inspired me to be proud of who I am. It's all we can be. My tenants and their families are all that I have. My novel is my journal in honor of all the "Granny Matties" of the world. It was another three years before both families moved into their first homes. It was the end of decades of change.

The grief and loss in my tenants' lives was overwhelming at times, yet they continued on, not knowing what the future held, clinging together with the belief that their faith would sustain them.

Watching them live their lives gave me, a simple building, the hope that I wouldn't be torn down or demolished before their stories were told. A grain of hope turned into reality because of my biographer, her research team, and "Fred's friends." My families provided a mosaic picture of generations from all over the world. Their tales are the tales of millions of Americans. Each tenant and their families' strong roots grew from seeds of hope—a legacy for current and future generations.

. . . .

CHAPTER TWENTY-TWO

Journey's End

W hen the Brown and Freeman families moved out of their apartment in 2002, I wanted them to stay and keep me company. Everything changed, and it was a lonely time. But I was grateful to be able to now watch, listen, and observe my one remaining tenant, eighty-two-year-old Mrs. Mandy Mixon. She was a World War II widow and lived here for twelve years. I always wanted to get to know her, but the Brown and Freeman families consumed all my attention.

Mrs. Mixon had only a few pieces of well-worn furniture in her neat little apartment. She loved her vintage 1940s Emerson wood cabinet tube radio and played it every day. Her large collection of books and photo albums were filled with happy memories of her family, and there was usually a pot of chicken soup or greens and beans cooking in the kitchen. It smelled delicious and was a familiar smell because the Browns and Freemans sometimes made the same food. Both families invited Mandy for dinner, but she constantly declined. Although at least three times a week, the Browns or Freemans delivered her a hot dinner, and she'd graciously thank them and promptly shut her door.

I heard her more than once tell her son Joshua that she would never move out of her apartment. He begged her to come and live with him and his family every time he visited her.

"Please let me be. I want to die at home, in my own apartment. I'm a tough old bird, and you need not worry about me. I've moved around all my life, and I'm spending the rest of my life right here in this apartment. I'm comfortable here, and the thought of moving is too overwhelming."

"But, Momma, we want you to be safe and with your family."

"I love all of you, but I can't." It's when I found out that Mandy never felt lonely. She felt her husband's spirit with her all the time. She knew he'd come and get her when the time came.

"Joshua, I love you, your wife, and my grandchildren, but I gotta stay where I feel at home. Please understand."

When I heard her say this, I knew why she would never move. Mandy helped me realize it's okay to be alone and not be lonely. Besides, the thought of my tenants' tales being told gives me comfort. Throughout Mandy's life, she made her own choices, only my choices are made for me. It's the way it is, and I can't change it. I know now that everyone feels lonely sometimes, especially when we think about our missing loved ones.

Every day I saw Mandy sitting in her kitchen chair looking out the window watching people and cars go by on Niagara Street. Often, a patrol car would pull up in front of my building. Officer Trudy would get out of her car and knock on Mandy's door while her partner waited with the engine running. "Mandy, need anything?" she'd say. Mandy would smile and say she was doing just fine. Then, Trudy would give her a sweet dessert and say, "Mrs. Mixon, here's my phone number. You call me if you need help. I'll stop by whenever I work the afternoon shift to check on you and the building."

She smiled back and quickly closed her door.

It felt good to know Mandy was being checked on because all I could do was hope she'd live a long time.

It wasn't long before vandals spray-painted the outside walls of my building. Then, I heard the windows being broken and police sirens pulling up in front of me. I was under attack. Why, I don't know. Mandy didn't seem worried, but her son was, and he begged her to come home with him. The answer stayed the same.

"No, I'm sorry, Joshua, I can't."

Then, one night in 2005, my brave Mrs. Mandy Mixon died peacefully in her sleep. I was devastated. She was my friend. Her wisdom saved me from feeling like a victim, and I'll always be grateful.

I've learned that in order to be alone at a certain point in your life you have to enjoy your own company. It's what Mandy did in her sunset years. She treasured her happy memories, and they sustained her until the day she died.

In my mind, I started to think that maybe my days were numbered too. The vandals continued to try to break into my building, and I was scared that one of them would set me on fire. Then, in 2012, an auctioneer arrived with a man who looked me over from the basement on up to the fourth floor. He even looked at my roof. I heard him say he bought me for $20,000 at an auction. I thought I was saved. Only it wasn't long before I realized I was still being neglected. Then, my new owner never came back, and I never found out what happened to him. I thought about my former tenants and how resilient they were in the face of adversity. I quickly stopped thinking negatively and decided not to give up hope, after all, I made it this far, and I'm not about to give up now.

A few days later, I heard my front door open and thought it might be another new owner. Only instead, it was a young woman with an empty knapsack on her back. She had a large flashlight and a notebook in her hand. I watched and wondered why the young woman was looking into the closets of my two second-floor apartments. It made me nervous because I was frightened that if she went into Bobby Mooney's old apartment, she might discover his closet with the secret box filled with evidence of our unusual friendship. All I could do was watch her. I saw her spend extra time in the first apartment's bedroom closet and had no idea why she was even in the building.

Then, she headed toward the second apartment's closet. I was panicky. All of a sudden, she discovered the loose floorboard in the closet. She pulled the rest of the board up and found the now fragile box filled with Bobby's notes and letters. I'll never forget this moment. I wanted to jump out of my wall and protect my most precious memory safely hidden until Bobby returned. She quickly emptied the box of notes and letters and put them in her knapsack and took them with her when she left. I couldn't believe it. What would Bobby say when he comes back?

I was fortunate to find out later that her name was Sylvia and she was a graduate student working on her master's thesis about apartment buildings built in Buffalo in the 1900s.

She always made it a point to look into each old building's bedroom closets because it was where she'd often find secret hiding places hidden beneath the closet floorboards. They often contained tiny empty boxes, photographs, and empty cloth bags. It was the reason she carried an empty knapsack with her just in case she found a hidden treasure. Her University of Buffalo Professor Dr. Rodgers gave her special permission to ask the owner if they could enter my building while the professor agreed to wait for Sylvia in each apartment's narrow hallway. What they found in the building was going to be their secret. The key would be returned the next day.

Little did I know, the role fate played in what happened next. I found out later that when Sylvia read through all Bobby Mooney's notes and letters, she realized the first letters were written by a little boy talking to a building named Fred in the 1950s. But then the young woman realized it was impossible. How can a building, named Fred, talk to a little boy? She saw how little Bobby Mooney continued writing until he graduated from high school and was drafted into the Vietnam War. Then, Sylvia read one of his last letters to Fred before he hid them in the closet for the last time. She found out that Bobby had just been accepted to the University of Buffalo with the goal of becoming a history professor right before he was drafted. She wondered if Bobby was able to achieve his goal and graduate from UB like she would be doing the following spring.

"I have to find Bobby Mooney," she told her professor with tears in her eyes. "I know buildings don't talk. But this one comes alive on these fragile papers. I feel destined to take him back to keep his promise to Fred." This was an unusual circumstance, and Sylvia's professor promised to keep it a secret, even though it was something she normally didn't do.

"Was it a coincidence that Professor Mooney was on her alumni list? Or was it destiny?" thought Sylvia. She had to find out the answer and have Bobby keep his promise to Fred. When she found out Professor Mooney lived a half-hour away from Fred, Sylvia reached out and called him several times before he finally agreed to meet with her.

When she pulled up in front of his house, she was nervous.

"Come in," he said. "I've been waiting for you. How are you?"

"I'm good now," Sylvia said, reaching into her knapsack. "Here are your notes and letters, Professor Mooney."

Bobby was shocked to see the yellowed papers she handed him. Then, his eyes filled with tears, and he looked confused.

"I can't believe this! I never expected to see them again. Thank you so much. Fred means everything to me." He took a step back when he realized what he just said. "You must think I'm strange, talking about a building like that."

"No, I don't. I totally understand. Please, let's go. I'll take you to him."

"Whew, are you sure it's not too late?"

"Please, Professor Mooney, if you don't return, it's possible that soon Fred will no longer exist."

"Okay, let's go, Sylvia. I'm going to keep my promise."

"Professor Mooney, I know that buildings don't talk and don't have names. But I know for sure that yours does and you're supposed to go see him like you promised. I can't wait until you meet Fred again. Please let me take you to him now."

"I'm sad just thinking about it. I didn't keep my promise. I hope I can handle it. I've attempted to go before but couldn't walk into the building, so I just stopped trying. It's the regret of my life."

Sylvia hugged him. Bobby lowered his head and then looked up at her. "He saved me from a life of miserable sadness. Our Chocolate Ladies, Hannah and Alice, took me in and gave me a home when I was homeless. They loved me like my family couldn't. You're right. I'm ready. I know he's still waiting for me. Thank you for finding me."

When she pulled up in front of me, Bobby took a few deep breaths before getting out of the car. Sylvia reached out, touched his hand, and said, "It's okay. Let's go, your friend, Fred, is waiting.

I'll wait for you outside in the hall. Then, she gave him a thumbs up. Here you go. Here's the key."

Bobby opened my front door, hesitated, and took another deep breath before entering my building. I heard the door open and thought it might be another new owner. I was surprised to see a tall, thin man with a full head of white hair enter Bobby's second-floor apartment closet. I thought I was dreaming.

"Fred, I'm Bobby. I've come back to keep my promise. Can you hear me? I'm sorry it wasn't sooner."

There was a long silence before he heard my voice in his mind and answered.

"Fred, I never forgot our friendship. You helped me grow up and become a strong man." Then, Bobby told me something I'll never forget. "Fred, you were a father to me." It was a moment of truth because when Bobby told me, I realized he was the son I've always wished I had.

We talked for what seemed like hours in the tiny closet. Bobby sat cramped on the floor with his long legs extended into the empty bedroom. I promised him that whenever he thinks of me, I'll be there in his mind, waiting to hear from him. I told him he will never be alone again, and I won't be either. I told him I'd go with him now, only I have to stay and find out what happens to me.

Bobby became quiet and reflective. "Fred, I know it's been your destiny to tell your tenants' stories."

Sylvia entered Bobby's old apartment just as our conversation was ending. Then, he introduced me to her, and she shared her story with me. As they left the apartment, Bobby turned and waved to me smiling, knowing we'd never again have to say goodbye. My wish was granted.

Lately, I've began thinking back on my life and the lives of my tenants and their families. I do know what life is like in the real world. For the past 120 years, I've had the privilege of living multiple lives vicariously in my mind. I'm keenly aware of their trials and tribulations and know how bendable truth is depending upon life's circumstances.

My firsthand adventure of many lifetimes has revealed the fact that we all have secrets we share with no one. I believe sometimes it's the only way we can cope with difficulties.

I know I exist to share the tales of past generations, and it is an honor. Their stories are held deep inside my consciousness. When my tenants first moved out, I was sad and hoped they'd come back and tell me about their lives.

But it's impossible to bring back time. If I didn't have good memories to remember, there would be nothing left to fill in the blanks. Freedom in America was important to all my tenants and their families. Its meaning inspired them to give up everything to have a better life for themselves, their children, and their children's children.

I've found out that freedom is worth the struggle to obtain. I'm older and wiser now and have heard multiple tenants describe their experiences facing discrimination. Many were misunderstood and alone in their struggle to be accepted. I saw how hard women fought for human rights and the right to vote. I know that inequality appears to come and go and often gets repeated generation after generation. It affected the lives of my immigrants, refugees, internal migrants, and descendants of enslaved people of Africa. It also happened to the past and many first-generation Americans.

I'm not a scholar, but one of the most important things I've learned is that leaders from all over the world have led their citizens into wars for all kinds of reasons, some large, some small, and some non-existent. They left followers and others to cope with their decisions, including some of my tenants who suffered major tragedies and losses. Their untold legacy and tales haunt me. I hope I can do justice to their lives.

In 2016, I was sold again for $130,000 as part of the West Side of Buffalo Renaissance. My inside walls were gutted, and the walls were refurbished. My developer put in new windows, a new water main, and is working on restoring the outside of my building to reflect how I originally looked.

It was shocking when I was sold again in June of the same year for $318,000. I was still afraid something terrible was going to happen to me. Fran was nervous too and often drove by and checked on me. I didn't lose hope because almost right across the street from me is a six million dollar remodeled and repurposed building, where young Bobby Mooney's father was employed at when his family first moved into my building in 1951.

Then, in 2020, my author experienced unexpected challenges in many areas of her life. I know I influenced her to stay true to my novel's authenticity, but there was one more shocking traumatic event that happened in our country and globally. It was the COVID-19 pandemic. And it was and is as brutal as the 1918 influenza pandemic, which spread rapidly during World War I.

I still remember the Consiglio father, Anthony, and son Sammy who were devastated when Maria, their two young daughters, and an unborn child lost their lives to the influenza pandemic. Their grief was overwhelming, and years later, their pain and anger turned into a tribute to their missing family. Please let their courage in the face of tragedy inspire you to honor your loved ones lost to the COVID-19 virus and help survivors to ease their pain.

It's now the end of 2020, and this current pandemic still affects everyone's lives, including mine.

My new Free Street Tavern, owner and operator, Joshua White had to close temporarily, and I can't wait until the pandemic is over.

Free Street Tavern located at 1469 Niagara Street, July 2020.
Courtesy of Joshua White, Tavern owner.

I pray and hope that the pandemic will be contained soon and that all my apartments are rented or leased. I've noticed recently that I have new tenants, and I can't wait to get to know them.

My life has come full circle, and my building preservation project is completed; my new residents will enjoy a great view of a revitalized Niagara Street, the Black Rock Canal, the Niagara River, and Canada.

I've discovered what helps all humans survive is an invisible thread of hope. I am grateful to still be standing tall in my building of dreams.

AFTERWORD

· · · · · · · · · · · · ·

My life changed forever in 2006 when an apartment building located on the corner of Niagara Street and Potomac Avenue talked to me. It was six years later before I could begin writing about Fred's story, mainly because I had to finish a book project. In October of 2012, the novice Orphan Building Research Team was organized. In a brief period of time, Patricia Smyton, Janet Mazzaroppi, and I knew we were in uncharted territory.

We had no historical research experience but were all dedicated to the process of uncovering the meaning of Fred's first words to me. *"Please tell my story before it's too late"* was the only clue we had to work with. Fred's plea for help became our mission.

At first, our adopted, humble, and sad-looking building didn't have a name. He was just building 1469. Now, we affectionately call him our friend Fred. For the past 120 years, Fred provided comfort to tenants from all over the world.

We learned quickly that historical facts are often subjective depending on cited research materials. The more we learned, the more we wanted to know. Slowly, characters emerged, decade upon decade. Fred's Friends provided us with personal reflections of their experiences in the neighborhood. Writing this novel gave me the opportunity to live his tenants' lives vicariously, experiencing the historical period they lived in. My characters came alive on the pages of this novel. My researchers listened to me talk about them and would often ask me, "Are these real people?" My answer was that they felt real to me. They inhabited my imagination based on our extensive research of Fred's history.

Librarians, historians, preservationists, and Fred's Friends helped us to move forward one step at a time. We investigated, questioned, and researched our research while tirelessly compiling factual information on one apartment building's history. Our first business card made us feel special because it was tangible evidence that we now considered ourselves official researchers.

The characters arrived in my mind only after hours and hours of reading and rereading our research. Who were they? How did they end up in this building? What was their life like? Why did they come to America? What time period did they live in? What were the consequences of their historical experiences? Most importantly, how does Fred want me to tell their stories?

Slowly, we learned the truth about Fred's architect and builder, including the story of Abigail, his first woman owner. The more we learned, the more we wanted to know why his story was important.

In the early 1900s, Buffalo, New York, was booming and the Canal District became a port of entry for many of Fred's first tenants. Throughout this novel, the demographics of the city and his building have changed dramatically. This novel focuses on the importance of the tenants he was able to observe. He learned their histories, felt their pain, and celebrated their successes. Fred gradually learned how people think and feel as human beings. His only regret was that most tenants never knew how much he loved and honored their strength, resilience, and courage.

Fred shared his reflections about his tenants' lives knowing he would never have one of his own, except on the pages of this book. All he could do was to find a writer's voice who would honor his culturally and ethnically diverse tenants.

I stopped by weekly at the gas station across the street from Fred. I always buy gas for my car and ask them if they have any updates on the new tenants who are gradually moving into his new apartment. How lucky I was that they both had so many stories to tell.

Sal and Joe have been Fred's loyal friends since the beginning of this project. I am grateful and thankful for their firsthand memories. It was often touch-and-go for Fred in the early twentieth century, and he was auctioned off twice and sold twice within a couple of years of finishing this novel. They always knew the inside scoop about the building's status.

Fred's name always had me questioning whether I found it out by chance or fate. It happened that a good friend's husband, Chet, played cards with the same small group of card players weekly. One night, for an unknown reason, he mentioned my name, and a special woman named Mary asked for my last name. She turned out to be a friend I hadn't seen in over forty years. We met and shared information about our lives. I told her about my latest writing project and let her know that the apartment building didn't have a name.

Suddenly, she stopped talking, looked me in the eye, and said, "Yes, he does. His name is Fred."

"How do you know?" I was incredulous.

"He just told me," she said, quietly. "It's something I've never told anyone. Ever since I was a young girl, I could look into the past. It scared me at first, and now that I'm an older woman, I hardly ever do it. I have to give you a message. He wants you to consider me his messenger throughout this project." It is exactly what I did bimonthly for years. Sometimes Mary told me to be quiet and listen, and I did.

This entire project has been a labor of love. Fred's legacy has been inspirational and has gathered support from individuals from all walks of life. What I've learned is that no matter what happens in our lives, past generations are the roots of strength and resilience for current and future generations.

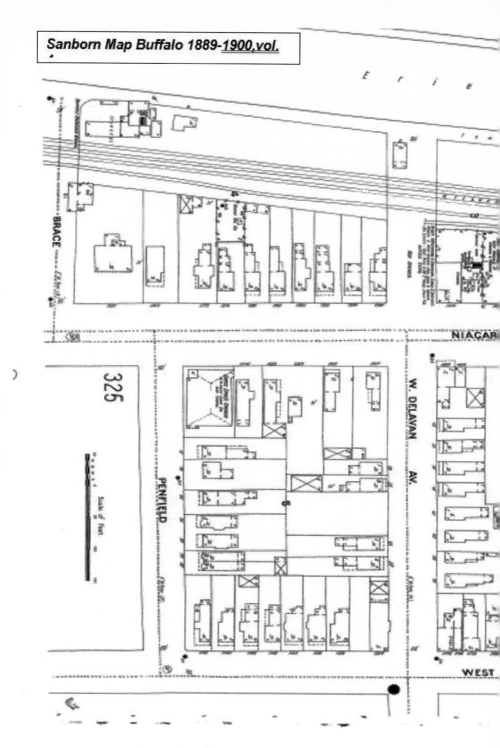

Sanborn Map Buffalo 1889–1900, Vol. 4 Sheet 327.
Buffalo Public Library, Research Databases.

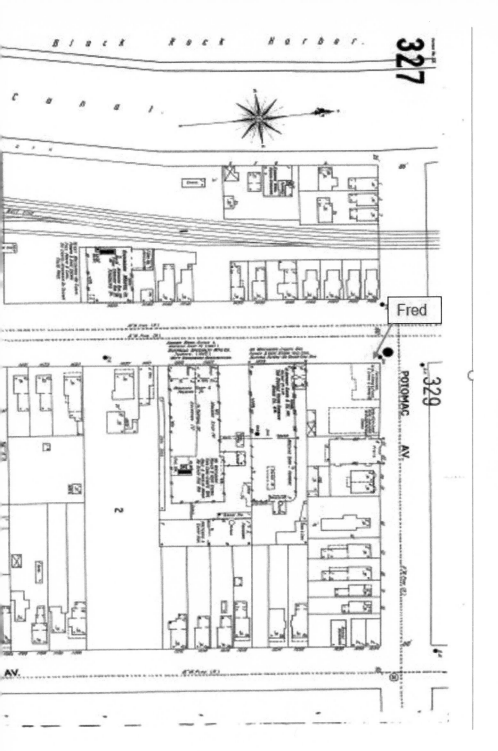

ACKNOWLEDGMENTS

Thank you to my entire family and extended families who graciously heard my passion regarding this long journey toward publication. I appreciate all friends and acquaintances who expressed an interest in this project, especially all the Back on Track Volunteers for their unconditional support. Also, I have to thank Joe Dileo, Editor of the *Per Niente* magazine, and Co-editor Joey Giambra, a remarkable man who recently passed away from COVID-19 in 2020, for printing my promotional tribute article to Sicilian immigrants.

A debt of gratitude and appreciation to my unbelievable Orphan Building Research Team members, Patricia Smyton and Janet Mazzaroppi, for their dedication to Fred and my work. They were both diligent professionals who provided me with excellent feedback, ideas, and suggestions during this entire project. A gigantic thank you to a dear friend and excellent typist, Jane Hauser, who excels on all levels. Her support, encouragement, and patience is admirable. She typed too many drafts to mention, always with a smile. Our entire team of four has experienced a remarkable journey back into the past to create a touchstone for the future.

Thank you to Jane Kilewald who edited my first rough draft and bravo to Jessica Gang, my first developmental editor, who taught me editing basics and gave me suggestions on how to proceed with the manuscript.

I want to express my gratitude to the many people who listened to the concept of this novel. They provided valuable feedback, support, and assistance during this nine-year process.

RESEARCH ACKNOWLEDGMENTS

. . . .

A note of appreciation to the Family Tree Restaurant and their welcoming staff who always allowed the Orphan Building Research Team to meet for hours at a time during extensive meetings. Another favorite restaurant was Santasiero's where we were welcomed and often met with a special group of "Fred's Friends" throughout this entire project, including a special thank you to Sharon our server. This restaurant was an important stop for Fred's tenants throughout the decades, especially during the Depression. Many survived hard times by eating their delicious food at a reasonable cost. John Brands Jr., the great-grandson of the founder, Dominic Santasiero, operates the restaurant for his mother, Phyllis Brands, and ensures his guests still receive food for a reasonable cost.

I'm extremely thankful to Salvatore J. Bonfante and his son, Joe Carm & Sal's Auto Service almost directly across the street from Fred. It's where I bought gas for my car at their station weekly and listened to the stories they told me about the people who lived in Fred's apartment building across the street. I was fortunate because they had many tales to tell. They have been Fred's loyal friends since the beginning of this unique project. Thank you both for your firsthand memories. Sal and Joe always knew the inside scoop about the building and willingly shared the details with me.

An additional thank you to Lou and Joe Saviano's barbershop for allowing our research team to see their unique collection of historical photographs. A special thank you also to Ted Marks of Fowler's Chocolates for sharing his notebook collection of pictures and articles about the history of their company and chocolate-making. I'm grateful that Fred's building was heart-bombed by a group of Young Preservationists on Valentine's Day in 2013 and their informing the public of his dire situation.

Our appreciation further extends to the staff of the Buffalo & Erie County Public Library and Grosvenor Library for teaching us how to find and use all of the important resources we needed. They included The Polk City Directories, Buffalo Address Books, Sanborn Fire Insurance Atlases, Ordnance Survey Maps, Children's Aid Annual Reports, Deed and Property Records including local history files, Federal and State Census Reports, Child and Family Service Records, New York State Death Records, and local newspaper archives.

Our research team thanks the Buffalo History Museum's staff for the use of their directories and excellent photograph collections. Another valuable resource was the Intensive Level History and Black Rock Tax Assessment Records, located in the City of Buffalo Inactive Records Center. Their staff was extremely helpful in teaching us how to interpret Fred's records.

An extended thank you to the multiple individuals we interviewed regarding their childhood memories of Fred and also the West Side of Buffalo. They were instrumental in helping characters come alive on the pages of this novel.

RESEARCH PROCESS

. . . .

In the fall of 2012, the Orphan Building Research Team began its historical fiction project using primary and secondary resources. Our team worked backward and forward, switching between resources to track Fred's history from 1900 through the end of 2020 for publication in 2021. Historical books and websites were of vital importance to set a realistic framework of Buffalo, New York, in the twentieth century.

Discovering the facts regarding the original construction of Fred's apartment building and the changes made over 121 years was a challenge. This nine-year project began with copies of two original pictures of the apartment building we think were in the 1940s and 1950s. Our research further identified all the businesses that were located on the first floor of the building.

Our research team discovered a wealth of demographic information, including tenant ages, ethnicity, and occupations. Over time, each fictitious character emerged from my imagination. Actual historical events inside and outside America were identified to allow me to recreate realistic events for each character and their families. Our research consisted of a multitude of historical resources, and we extend a special thank you to the Church of Latter-Day Saints

Family History Center and their welcoming staff for their excellent assistance and guidance.

The D'Youville College Archives took us back in time starting in 1908. Their records helped me to learn what it was like for young women attending college over a century ago.

Many historical books were reviewed several times, helping me learn about Buffalo's early history. They included three books written by Mark Goldman: *City on the Lake: The Challenge of Change in Buffalo, New York 1990*; *City on the Edge, Buffalo, New York, 1900–2007*; and *High Hopes: The Rise and Decline of Buffalo, New York, 1993*. They were significant to understanding the roots of Buffalo. *America's Crossroads: Buffalo's Canal Street/Dante Place; The Making of a City*, authored by Michael N. Vogel and Paul E. Redding and edited by Edward J. Patton and Elizabeth Foy was a valuable and constant resource regarding life in the Canal District in the 1900s and its effect on new immigrants to America. Additional books included: *Strangers in the Land of Paradise: The Creation of an African American Community, Buffalo, New York 1900–1940* written by Lillian S. Williams in 1999, *Children of the Settlement Houses*, written by Caroline Arnold in 1998 and *Immigrant Kids*, by Russell Freedman, originally published in 1980.

Significant historical websites provided us with a wealth of information and included: The Ancestry Library, The Library of Congress, Canadian Genealogy, Western New York Heritage Press, The Buffalonian, Buffalo Research, Buffalo History Index, Excerpt: John W. Percy, The Erie Canal: From Lockport to Buffalo, Buffalo Architecture, and the Circle Association's African American History of Western New York State 1900–1935.

AUTHOR BIO

· · · · · · · · · · · · ·

Frances R. Schmidt

Fran has a passion for people and an enthusiasm for their personal histories. In this first novel, *FRED: Buffalo Building of Dreams*, she uses her storytelling skills to help FRED impart the compelling tales of the tenants and their families who called him their home for over more than a century. It is an imaginative and well-researched slice of history as told by a humble apartment building. FRED's intimate observations reveal to him (and to us) what it means to be human.

With possible demolition looming, Fran's goal was to tell the building's tales before it was too late. Her promise to FRED has been achieved, and it has been an extraordinary experience that changed her life forever. She has learned the importance of historical accuracy and the truths it can reveal.

The novel was honored to be selected for a first chapter professional reading on the Novel Writing Festival website (August 2020).

Fran is a retired director of a Buffalo, New York, college career counseling center. Stemming from that experience, Fran has authored two well-received job search books, *Getting Hired, Handbook for College Graduates* and *Getting Hired in any Job Market*, and several related articles. Once again helping people to tell their stories.

Fran was the past founder and coordinator of an all-volunteer Back on Track Career Peer Mentoring Program for the Society of Saint Vincent de Paul of WNY from 2000–2017.

Fran Schmidt resides in the Western New York region.

Find out more about Fran—and FRED—on her website: https://francesrschmidt.com

Frances R. Schmidt